MENTOR

Duncan Jefferson

ALSO BY
Duncan Jefferson

Mr. Dickens

Camino Salvado: A Pilgrimage

Captain Scully

THE RENAISSANCE BROTHERS SERIES:

The Butcher's Boy

The Young Countess

The Missing

Contents

Preface

WHEN I FIRST arrived in Australia, most English expats were arriving as '£10 Poms' – a colloquial term used to describe British citizens who migrated to Australia in the post-World War II period. My wife and I chose to pay our own way... just in case we didn't like the place. But we fell in love with it and are honoured to call Australia our home.

However, when we landed in Victoria back in the 1970s I was taken aback by the apparently affectionate greeting of, "G'day, you Pommy bastard." I was quickly informed that this was a much kinder epithet than 'whingeing Pom', in which case I may as well have turned around and gone back!

I mention this because *Mentor* is set in the late 1960s, an era when such descriptions were in common use, along with 'wog', 'wop' and 'boong'. At that time, in the majority of cases, they were used with great affection towards Italian, Greek or Aboriginal mates. Nowadays, such terms are rightly seen as culturally demeaning and disrespectful to fellow Australians, so I apologise to anyone who may be offended by the use of such terms in this book. This is a story grown out of that era and as such I have used the vernacular of the time.

But first and foremost, this is a story inspired by a real life Kev, a quintessential Australian bloke and a man who in his own way has been a mentor for myself, our family and for so many others.

Dedicated to K.O'B.

Divine intervention

GROPING MY WAY out of a deep sleep, the first thing I became aware of was the smell of vinegar. I tried to lick my dry lips, but my tongue felt as if it had been through a mincer. Having decided that such information was too much for my foggy mind to deal with, I opened my eyes to check out what was going on in the outside world.

A pretty nurse was standing at the side of my bed, focusing on a silvered column of mercury as it bobbed its way down a glass tube. She was measuring my blood pressure. When you've watched as many episodes of *Doctor Kildare* as I have, then you know such details. I shifted slightly in the bed and instantly became aware of new pain, this time in my backside.

"Ah, so you've finally decided to join us, have you?" the nurse said, her eyes reflecting her pleasure at my return to consciousness. I detected a slight Irish lilt, but that's not unusual up here in the bush. Before I could answer, a groan came from the bed next to me. Reluctantly shifting my gaze away from the nurse, I turned my head to see Chook Harris. He looked different to the last time I'd seen him. His nose seemed flatter and both his eyes were black, swollen and closed.

"Sorry," the nurse interrupted me, "but we couldn't find anywhere else to put him. We're full. It's the footy season, remember?" Seeing the confused look on my face, she went on. "You don't remember what happened?" My blank look confirmed her suspicions. "And you've never had any fits before?" she asked, as if every man and his dog had fits.

"Never," was all I could muster before my minced tongue caused me to baulk at any more conversation. I nodded in Chook's direction.

"Seems like you've got some decent friends, Tel. Mr Harris here has suffered from a severe dose of divine retribution." Her eyes danced playfully and I felt normal service return to certain parts of my anatomy. "But you need to rest. Doctor will be in to see you shortly. By the way, your mum said to say she'll be in at lunch time. She had to get back to the shop," she added, tucking the sheets so tightly under the mattress that I could barely breathe. This girl was stronger that her slight frame suggested. My spirits were positively bursting out of me, which apparently manifested itself in the look I gave her. "I think it's time you had a rest, mi' young boyo," she said firmly, before checking her watch and leaving the small two-bed ward at Yarramah District Hospital.

I lay there staring at the ceiling, listening to the sound of the phone thrum at the nurses' station just down the corridor. How the hell did I get here? Fragments of history began to form in my mind. I tried to fit them back together.

There was a girl – of course there was a girl: I love ALL girls. Hey, I grew up in a Greek family, and it's a well-known fact that Greek men were placed here on earth with the sole intention of loving women. OK, I was just sixteen but the ancient Spartans were seasoned warriors by the time they were my age. And it was a man's duty to protect women, isn't it?

As the fog cleared from my memory, it turned out that Julie was the particular woman I was sent here to protect … well, she was more of a girl than a woman. Julie was a little stocky and wore wire-framed glasses that made her face look like she'd just been pinched on the BTM (in our house we we're not allowed to say 'bum'. According to Mum, 'bum' is a bad word, though just about everyone else at high school said bum, and most used far worse language than that!)

Julie's a nice girl and I knew she liked me. It was something to do with the olive skin and brown eyes that attracted the girls, or maybe it was my blonde curly hair. Sure, Greeks didn't normally have blonde hair, but for all

I knew I may have been a Dutchman! Because, you see, I'm adopted. Mum preferred to say 'chosen', but it was all the same to me. Due to the quirks of biology, I didn't have any half-brothers or sisters so there'd been no competition for my parents' love and attention. All in all, life had been really sweet for me and as a consequence, up until that moment I'd been one very happy camper.

But back to remembering what'd happened!

I'd been walking home from the shop. My dad, Peter, owned the fruit and veggie shop in Lisle Street, and being the only one in town it was a full on job. The downside was that he had to drive down to the markets in Melbourne twice a week to pick up the fresh stuff. The 400-kilometre round trip meant he had to leave at four o'clock in the morning in order to complete the journey in daylight. Once home, he then had to unload and stack his stock before it got dark. Luckily, during school time I got let off going with him, but in the holidays it played havoc with my beauty sleep!

Just outside of O'Ryan's Cement Works I'd caught up with Julie and we were chatting about this and that. I remembered that I could hear the music coming from Mr O'Ryan's transistor radio and the guttural growl of his cement mixer in the background, then suddenly I got a shove on the shoulder.

"Bloody wogs, can't you think of anything else apart from shagging girls?" The smell of grog on Chook's breath would have stunned an ox.

Most people tried to avoid Chook when he was in that sort of state, but my attention was elsewhere. "Out of the way, kid," he went on, pushing me to one side. "Let a real man finish the job." With that, he made a grab for Julie.

I steadied myself and pushed him back. "Back off, Mr Harris. Go home. You're drunk." He stared back at me furiously. The radio and the cement mixer played on in the background.

"You little bastard," he shouted and aimed a punch at my head.

That's all I remembered. Apart from one strange thing … there was another sound mixed in there somewhere. I had heard the call of an owl.

"Your mum's here to see you, Tel" my Irish beauty informed me from the doorway. As she stepped back to allow Mum in, I caught sight of her face in profile – black hair trying to escape from under her nurse's hat, fresh red cheeks and a slightly upturned nose, which gave her the look of a grown-up leprechaun.

"You a big bad bastard, Mr Harris," were the first words my mum said. That almost floored me again. It was the first time I had ever heard my mum swear. Boy, she must have been really mad. Luckily for Chook, he was still semi-conscious and missed the threat. But I reckon if it came to the biff, Mum would give Chook a decent going over. When you spent half your day lifting full crates of spuds and cabbages, you definitely put on a bit of condition even if you're a girl. Or in Mum's case, a sturdy Greek woman who believes that feeding her men lots of good food was the Eleventh Commandment.

"My poor boy, what did this bad man do to you?" she said, running her thick finger over my even thicker lip.

"She'll be right, Mum. Nurse here reckons the lip'll make me more attractive," I said, checking the doorway to see if she'd overheard. She had, but she didn't let on. I liked that! "Mind you, I've got a cracker of a lump on the back of mi' noggin', and for some reason a bigger pain in mi' bu…" I was about to mention the 'magic' word before I corrected myself and said, "Buttocks."

"What is this buttock, Telemecus?" Yep, it had to come out sometime. My real name was Telemecus Alysandratos, first and only son of Peter and Nana Alysandratos, proprietors of the Fresh Fruit and Vegetable Store, Lisle Street, Yarramah.

I rolled over and pointed to my rear end. "Must've landed heavily or something," I muttered. At that moment my pretty nurse reappeared with a wiry, older man wearing a sports jacket. He made a beeline for my bed. It was Doc Buckley. He gave a nod of recognition to Mum before opening the chart the nurse was carrying for him.

The thin manila folder carried the story of my life in Yarramah. Although I didn't know where I'd been born, the rest of my significant medical milestones were recorded in the local hospital. I'd been circumcised there – although thankfully I had no recognition of that particular moment in my life – had my broken wrist fixed there when I came off my bike aged six, had my appendix removed there in my early teens, and now had myself a bed there after being flattened by Chook Harris when I was sixteen. To a country boy that seemed a full and exciting life; if only I'd known what was before me.

"How are you feeling?" Dr Buckley said, looking up from the folder through his half-moon glasses. He had a thin face surmounted by a bulbous nose. But it was the bushy eyebrows arching high above his spectacles like two lost, hairy caterpillars that demanded one's fullest attention. I may have been guessing, but the right one seemed far more active than the left one.

"A bit sore, Doc," was my timid reply.

"Never had any fits, faints or funny turns before?" my medical inquisitor asked.

"Not that I know of," I replied, looking up at Mum to see if I'd answered correctly.

"What is this 'funny turn', Dr Buckley?" she demanded.

The good doctor went all sheepish; my mum can have that effect on men. I think it may have something to do with the size of her. Dr Buckley filed his fist across his stubbly chin, searching for an easy answer.

"Convulsions aren't that uncommon after a blow to the head. That's what seems to have happened to your son."

I glanced at the nurse. Her pretty grin had been replaced by a very professional expression. My lust levels suddenly plummeted. I didn't feel happy with the direction this conversation was headed. Dr Buckley glanced down at his lap and brushed off an invisible spot from his trousers. "From what Jim Watt, the ambulance officer told me, it appears that you had a full-blown fit. You'd bitten your tongue and…" He paused as if for effect, but I think it may have been more out of embarrassment for me. "You were incontinent of urine, as well."

A baffled silence descended. Neither Mum nor I had a clue what he'd meant. I decided to break the ice: "Huh?"

The silence continued as eyes darted from one to the other before a light bulb went off in my head. "Did I piss mi' pants?" I blurted out before I had time to think. For once, Mum's arm didn't even twitch in my direction. Geez, this must have been serious.

"So why's mi' bum sore, Doc?" This time I got 'the look'. "Sorry, Mum," I mumbled.

Dr Buckley came and sat on the side of my bed and I felt compassion oozing out of him. Behind that strict, stern front was a really kind man. "Well, Tel, when you were brought in you had another fit and I had to give you an injection of paraldehyde to stop it. It's not a very pleasant injection, and that's why we give it in the buttocks."

"Does it smell like vinegar?" What a stupid question to ask but it was what came into my head. "When I woke up that's the first thing I can remember." Doc nodded, indicating that I'd guessed correctly. I glanced up at Mum, my head empty of all reasonable thoughts and hers obviously seething with questions but unsure how to frame them in a foreign tongue. "So, when can I go home?" I finally asked. At least that cheered the good doctor up. He was back on firm ground with that one.

"All being well, you can go home tomorrow, but I will need to see you again next week as I need to run a few tests."

Like most people who go to the doctors, my brain immediately latched onto the good news, while letting the sting in the tail of what he had just said fly right over my head. "Thanks, Doc," I replied and returned my attention to the good-looking nurse. I think she smiled at me, but it was one of those 'you poor sod' sort of looks and definitely not what a hormone-fuelled Greek boy was hoping to see.

"Excuse me, Doc," I said as Dr Buckley was beetling out of the room, "but what happened to Chook? I didn't do that, did I?"

Bill Buckley, respected member of the community, president of the golf club and a man as morally straight as an arrow, attempted to suppress a wicked grin. "No, Tel, it wasn't you. I believe he ran into Kevin O'Ryan." Having made this announcement, he turned and left, with Mum close on his heels. Confused by the good doc's answer, I looked at the nurse. Her eyes were now fairly sparkling with impish delight. Without answering my unspoken question, she too turned and left. I was left alone with my thoughts and the sound of Chook snoring loudly and occasionally grimacing before he let off a loud fart. The man was an animal.

Fit for nothing

THINGS DIDN'T GO well after that. I thought it'd just be a simple case of going home and slotting straight back into my normal routine – helping Dad in the shop before school, going to school, hanging out with my mates after school and then going home to help out in the shop again. Then there were the important extras, like finding time to kick a footy, dreaming about becoming a champion surfer – which is a bit of a challenge when you live 350 kilometres from the sea – and most important of all, dreaming about girls!

But it didn't work out like that.

I felt really listless and began to have headaches on a regular basis. I also had another fit.

One evening, I'd gone with Dad to drop off a delivery to a farmer out at Curramine. On our way back, we drove past a row of trees planted by one of the cockies back around the time of the Boer War, or so the legend goes. People who plant trees generally don't have any imagination. They regiment them rather than plant them, which is something Mother Nature would never consider doing, even in one of her blackest moods. Anyway, as we drove by, the sunlight was flickering through the gaps between the trees and out of the blue, I heard that owl again. The next thing I knew, Dad was frantically shouting at me to see if I was alright. As the fog left my brain I felt that unforgettable feeling of warmth in my pants – I'd pissed myself again.

Back at the hospital, Doc Buckley had his serious face on as he gave me the once over. It was one of those real deal examinations – none of this open your mouth and say 'ah' stuff; this was strip off to your undies and do all sorts of ridiculous things like touch your nose and then one of Doc's fingers, stand on one leg with your eyes shut, and get hit with a rubber hammer to make your arms and legs twitch.

"Everything appears normal," he said, but it didn't seem to make the man any happier. I looked at my dad, who looked just as relieved as I was at hearing those words.

From then on, though, it was man's business as the two of them discussed my life as if I wasn't even in the room. Listening to them talk, it seemed that my recent happy dreams about the future had rapidly transformed into a nightmare.

"Peter," Doc began, "I think Tel has grand mal epilepsy. It might've been caused by his recent head injury or it may be that the injury has triggered an underlying predisposition to epilepsy; whatever the reason, he needs treatment and he needs medication to reduce the chances of having further seizures. My suggestion is that I start him on a medication today, and in the meantime I will contact a neurologist over at the Base Hospital in Karrangamah and arrange an appointment for Tel to be seen as soon as possible."

My dad is a very smart man. Most of us Greeks are. Just because he runs a fruit and veg business, that doesn't mean he's got a head as dense as a pumpkin. Dad can speak three languages as well as English, he knows more about ancient Greek history than most professors at university and he's better with money than most accountants. But he's also one of those 'deep Greeks'. He's a thinker and a watcher. Behind those dark brown eyes and that black drooping moustache lies a humble, intelligent and very good man.

"Bill, what will this mean for Telemachus?" he asked. "Will the medicines affect his ability to study, play sport or work?"

"Good question, Peter," the doctor replied. "The short answer is probably yes, but we won't really know until he's started the medications to control the fits. What we do know is that medications like this, which work on the brain, will probably make him feel a little more tired than usual." Like the polished performer that he was, Doc removed his glasses, cleaned then studiously and then replaced them underneath his somewhat subdued caterpillars.

I wondered why Doc had used the royal we. Had he spoken to someone else about me? Was there something else 'they' were thinking about? Maybe an operation that might fix me up? The other thing I latched onto was the 'probably' bit. Sadly, experience has since taught me that doctors use the royal we to take the pressure off themselves, and 'probably' is a total furphy – what it really means is that it's dead set that those side effects are going to happen.

"The other thing, which I know he won't like, is that he's off all sport until he's seen the specialist. As for the future, we'll have to wait and see." Bill Buckley looked across at me while reaching deep into his pocket. I watched those two hairy larvae on his forehead undulate into action.

"So, can I go the Year 12 dance next month?" was the only logical thing I could think to ask. The good doctor smiled and we all relaxed a little.

"I don't see why not, but do inform your dancing partner that there's a remote possibility you may display a few new steps she's never seen before."

"Can this be fixed or will Telemecus have to stay on medications for the rest of his life?" Dad was always coming up with an intelligent question, even though I really didn't want to hear the answer to this one. Doc almost writhed on the baited question Dad had just floated in front of him.

"Look, Peter, in my experience these seizures are often well controlled by medication and there are new and better treatments coming along all the time. Let's wait and hear what the specialist has to say." Dad held his gaze for a few milliseconds and in that time learned the truth. His son had epilepsy: there wasn't a lot anyone could do, and he'd have to live with it for the rest of his life.

Dr Buckley was as good as his word and I saw the specialist the following week. Not that it made a whole deal of difference. He basically did the same things as Doc had done, plus a few more. He confirmed what Dr Buckley had already said and he booked me in for a thing called an EEG – in medical parlance it's called an electroencephalograph – which proved to be the final confirmation of my doom.

I had grand mal epilepsy. Shut the book, I was stuffed big time!

From the first day I began my medication, I descended into a mental fog. Everything slowed down. Everything was an effort and everyone was sickeningly sycophantic towards me. I couldn't be bothered to go out, I felt tired all the time and my only refuge was in Mum's cooking, which meant that I really stacked on the weight. The only glimmer of sunshine was that Julie called past the shop, and for the first time I thought she looked quite pretty. She wasn't wearing her glasses, which made her face look totally different, although she seemed to be blinking far more than before.

"Have you got something in your eye, Jules?" I asked stupidly.

"No, you duffer, I've got contact lenses. It's the first time I've worn them. What do you think?" She brushed an imaginary stray strand of hair away from her face.

"I think you look really pretty," I replied, before picking up the remains of some souvlaki and polishing it off to hide my embarrassment.

"Are you going to the school dance?" Her question startled me.

"Not sure," I mumbled. "Maybe."

"I've got a cousin with epilepsy and he's incredible." In a flash she had my full attention. How did she know? Did she know? Where was this going? "He takes me for rides on his dirt bike around the property. He hasn't had a fit for ages so his doc said it was OK to drive."

Talk about swirling emotions! A conga line of questions filed into my mind. I was about to ask something when Julie picked up a bunch of rosemary and crushed the stem between her fingers. The air was immediately filled with its essence.

"Maybe I could have the pleasure of the first dance? I was going to ask Julie Christie but she won't answer her phone."

"You're a dag, Tel. I'll have to check my dance card though. Steve McQueen's already asked me, but I don't reckon he's all he's cracked up to be so I'm sure I'll be able to make a space for you." She reached forward and kissed me on the cheek.

In an instant, it was goodbye to epilepsy and welcome back to a Greek teenager. Taking a step toward her, I was about to say something meaningful to this newfound wonder in my life, but like Fred and Ginger, as I stepped forward she stepped back.

"I have to go now. I'll see you at the dance. See ya, Tel." And with that she was gone.

Women!

The wrong steps

SCHOOL DANCES ARE scary places. First you have to escape the giggling heroes behind the toilets coughing their lungs up after sharing an illicit ciggy. "Fancy a drag, Tel?" one callow youth offered.

"No thanks, Fuzz. You know what, it's a strange thing, but I'd rather inhale the glorious perfume of some lucky girl's hair than suck the smoke from rolled up burning leaves."

"Tosser."

Just goes to prove that not every race has the soul of a poet, like we Greeks have.

Entering the maw of the gymnasium was not classic Hollywood material. Firstly, the smell of teenage perspiration impregnated the air, and secondly, instead of the sweeping sounds of a stringed orchestra setting the scene for a romantic tryst, we had the brassy sounds of Knobby Clarke's jazz ensemble. All this was heightened by Mrs Lyons' famous non-alcoholic fruit punch served in a soup tureen. But salvation came in the unexpected form of Goggs, who'd slyly purloined his old man's hip flask and filled it with vodka. Needless to say, it certainly added some zip to Mrs L's fruity wonder.

On one side of the hall stood the girls, totally transformed from their schoolyard appearance to, on the most part, gorgeous young women. It's amazing what a bit of lippy, some nice perfume and a pretty dress can do to even the most average of the female species. Unfortunately, you couldn't say the same for the desultory creatures lined up on the other side of the hall. Most of my mates were pretty awkward around girls at the best of time, but now they looked beyond redemption in their father's hand-me-down finery: most of it of a muddy brown hue and all of it ill fitting!

I was lucky. Dad, despite working in a shop all his life, was actually a pretty snappy dresser. His wardrobe contained three fine suits which he rarely had a chance to wear. Unfortunately, I happened to be a couple of inches taller than him, which would have made me look like a complete idiot if I'd worn his trousers: but then Kath Donnelly stepped in. "No problems, Tel. I'm let them down a bit and you'll be the Prince Charming and beau of the ball all rolled into one."

"Aw, Kath. You're a genius," I'd said, attempting to get my arms all the way around her ample frame. Her throaty chuckle wobbled the dewlap under her chin and gently rocked us both.

"I've always had a soft spot for good-looking young Greeks." Even Mum laughed at that.

So there we were in the school gym, lined up on either side of the hall – girls on the left and blokes on the right. The big question was, who was going to be the first one to walk across no-man's-land and get the show on the road?

Naturally, being a Greek, I had no compunction about stepping into that void. I kept my eyes firmly on where Julie was standing in the midst of a small flock of her friends and made a beeline for her.

"Shall we show them how to dance, Jules?"

Her eyes flashed in all directions, while the chatter on her side of the hall reduced perceptibly. She looked at me, her eyes creasing into a complicit grin before she answered, "Certainly, sir," and, giving a slight bend of her knee, took my hand and allowed me to lead her onto the dance floor. After that, it was like the fall of Troy, with both sides spilling into the void as Knobby's mob gave it their best shot. Things really began to hum.

Almost immediately, the combination of Goggs' vodka, Mrs L's fruit punch, the epilepsy medication and my frenetic dance style combined to cause a very unpleasant, bilious sensation in my stomach.

"Sorry Jules," I blurted, "but I think I'm going to throw up." With that I headed for the exit and deposited my tea in a small garden bed near the school fence.

"Are you OK?" Julie asked in a concerned fashion, having followed me outside.

"Couldn't be better," I replied with heavy sarcasm. "Can't dance, can't play sport, in fact there's not bloody much I can do these days, so yeah, life is real sweet." I swung my jacket over my shoulder and headed off home.

"Want me to walk you home?" Julie asked in a plaintive voice.

"Thanks for asking, but I'll be fine." Geez, I really carried on like a pork chop.

As I crossed Barrett Park, the moonlight caught the white bark of a ghost gum tree. Even though I'd seen the tree a thousand times, it always made me slow down and admire its beauty. Tonight, a large barn owl stood on one of the lower branches and watched me with its huge black eyes. It didn't make a sound, just bored its eyes into me until I was out of sight.

"You're home early," Dad said in surprise. "Dance finished already?"

"No, it's still going. I threw up in the school grounds and decided it was best to come home. Must have been Mrs L's fruit punch." I downed a glass of cold water from the tap. "I think I'll head off to bed. Thanks for the suit Dad. I reckon Julie and I were the best-looking couple on the dance floor tonight." I tried to sound brave but I felt pathetic. Leaving my parents to draw their own conclusions, I went to bed.

It wasn't a good night for sleeping.

Over the next few days I felt like I was dropping down into a deep dark well, which I had neither the energy nor the insight of how to get out of. Dad worked and worked but all the time I knew he was watching me. And Mum, bless her, kept on feeding me!

"Telemachus," Dad said one day "You need to do something with your head. It's turning into mush."

"It's the tablets, Dad," I pleaded. "Even if I wanted to think anything it's just to bloody hard to hold onto even one single thought!"

"Telemachus!"

"Sorry, Mum. But my brain feels like glue. Everyone looks at me as if I'm some sort of weirdo who at any second's going to throw up or fall over and froth at the mouth like some rabid dog. I can't do the things I want to do and in all truth, life just feels too bloody hard."

There was no remonstration from the good woman. She just turned to the sink and attacked the washing up with a vengeance. Looking across at her, it seemed to me as if her shoulders shook a little. "And I know how hard you guys are trying to protect me and I know that it's killing you, too. Perhaps you'd both be better off without me."

Dad glanced briefly in Mum's direction before coming over to me and grabbing me by the shoulders. "Don't you ever say that again, Telemachus. Your mum and I love you, despite yourself. We've loved you ever since you arrived in our world. Nothing will ever stop that love. Nothing."

"But you're not my real parents," I blurted, and immediately regretted it. I loved those guys so much and it was brutal of me to try and wound them like that, but I was hurting so much I wanted them to understand the pain I was going through.

"You are our son, Telemachus, and you always will be," Dad said softly.

"I'm sorry," I mumbled, and we both hugged each other before approaching the sink to envelop Mum in a group embrace.

Later on that day I was wandering along Lisle Street, past O'Ryan's Cement Works. The mixer was in full spate with the radio inside inviting me to "*Let's go surfing, surfing safari...* " – it was as if the musical gods were urging me to take a break and go to the beach.

"G'day, Tel," came the voice of Kevin O'Ryan from the shadow of his factory. The sun was waning but it must have been almost 40 degrees inside the corrugated iron walls of O'Ryan's. Kev's light blue singlet had dark blue stains down the front from the rivers of sweat running from his face and neck. His stubby football shorts revealed powerful but bowed legs, spattered with white blobs of drying cement. His muscular arms were trowelling off one of the cement posts lying flat in its mould and suspended upon two old wooden trestles. Kev had short cropped hair and fair, freckled skin which should have never left Ireland for Australia. To those who didn't know him, the man exuded intimidation. But to those whom he liked, there wasn't a better friend in the world.

"Grab us a shovel of mix, Tel," Kev said in a matter-of-fact way, although his gimlet eyes watched my every move just as a cat watches a mouse. Without giving it another thought, I wandered over to his cement barrow, grabbed the old ballast shovel that was leaning against it, and lifted out the mix as ordered. For the first time in ages I didn't think about myself, I just did as I was told. Kev had that mysterious knack of imbuing courage into people even though, truth be told, most people were just a tad scared of him.

"You've stacked on the weight, Tel. Mrs A been feeding you too much of that Greek tucker, eh?" Even while speaking, he never ceased from trowelling the fast-drying concrete post.

"No, Mr O'Ryan," I began, "it's the medications I gotta take. The doc said it might make me put on a bit of weight."

"A bit!" Kev shouted. "I reckon you'd give Sonny Liston a run for his money!"

I stood there leaning on the shovel while Kev punished his body in that overpowering heat. I glanced at the floor around his feet, glistening white with the dried-out salt from his sweat.

"Bit of an expert at leaning on shovels, eh?" he said sarcastically. I immediately went to put it back where I'd found it. "I never took you for being shy of work, son," he added. *"There's a new world somewhere beyond the promised land..."* played on his little radio.

Kevin looked across at another set of trestles and several empty moulds. "You'd be doing me a favour if you'd set those up for me. The quicker I can knock this off, the sooner I can get home for mi' tea." It was a well-known fact that Kev boarded at the Royal Hotel on Lisle Street, which meant that Kev took his 'tea' ice cold, with just a hint of hops, in a tall glass surmounted with a foamy head! Seeing as the licensing laws were pretty strict and hotels were only allowed to sell beer between the hours of 5 and 6 – popularly known as 'the swill' – it was highly unlikely that Kev would waste good drinking time by finishing off a few concrete posts.

"Hard work never hurt anyone, Tel, and there's nothing like an ice cold VB to wash down the dust at the end of a day." He smiled, revealing what was probably another of the reasons that most people were frightened of Kev – his teeth. Those that he still had seemed to come at you from different directions, giving him a slightly unhinged visage.

Half an hour later the two of us walked down the road to the Royal, sporting our matching sweat-soaked shirts. I hadn't felt this good since before I'd had my first fit.

"When do school holidays start, Tel?" he asked, although I sensed he knew very well that they began in a couple of weeks. I told him the dates. "If you're interested, I could do with an extra pair of hands. You're not a bad sort, and you're not a bad toiler either once you stop leaning on your shovel! Mind you, I can't promise that I'll pay you much ... and you might learn some terrible habits from me..." I looked askance at him and he gave one of his malicious yet endearing grins in return.

"Ask your dad and mum, and if they're game, just drop past the yard sometime and let me know." With that, he entered the Royal via the kitchen entrance and disappeared in the direction of the public bar.

When I reappeared at the shop, Dad was serving the last of the evening customers and generally tidying up around the place. He saw me come in but made no comment. I went out the back and began to stack some empty crates for him. He followed me in and eyed my cement-splattered shoes. "How's Mr O'Ryan?" he asked.

"He's asked me if I'd like to work for him over the summer holidays, Dad. That OK with you?"

"Pass me those cases of carrots, son," he said as he digested the idea. After he'd settled the carrots back into the cool room he turned, placed his arm around my shoulder saying, "It's fine by me, Telemachus, but I'm not sure what your mum's going to say." We didn't have to wait long to find out.

"No way," she shouted, "that Kevin O'Ryan is mongrel dog. He drink, he fight and..." her voice faltered, "he not nice to the young ladies," which was her way of saying that Kev was a bit of a stallion!

I knew well not to argue with her because that only made her more fixed in her thinking. Dad and Mum had been married for many years and he could read her like a book. So it was later on, while we were having our evening meal together, he casually mentioned that I was looking better than I had for some weeks and that a bit of hard work might be good for me. That was met with a flashing look from Mum, but she didn't say anything, which in itself was a good sign. Later on over the washing up he said that having some extra money coming in over the summer months could be a real help. Silence. Things were looking positively optimistic. Dad's a genius in these things!

The next morning he told me that he and Mum had had a chat after I'd gone to bed, and they thought that it was OK for me to tell Mr O'Ryan that I could work for him. That was, if he still wanted me to. "But don't bring any of his bad habits home with you, Telemachus, otherwise it's over."

"Thanks, Dad," I said and gave him a big hug.

I ran up the street before school to Kev's works and found him trowelling cement into one of the fence post moulds; the mixer was doing its daily job and his little tranny radio was tuned into a horserace from somewhere in New South Wales. "They're all crooks," he declared, nodding in the direction of the radio without breaking his rhythm.

"G'day, Mr O'Ryan," I began. "I asked Dad and Mum last night about working for you over summer and they said it's fine!"

Those gimlet eyes of his bored into me. "Your mum said it was ok?" he asked.

"Absolutely."

"Okey dokey," he said, "but I don't want you going home whingeing that it's hard yakka, or that your girlfriends complain that the skin on your hands has gone rough and hard." He stared me down before hustling me out, with, "No point being late for school as well, is there?" as he flicked the point of his trowel in the direction of the high school just up the road.

That evening, as Dad was checking through a recent consignment of fresh figs and discarding any that were too crushed to sell, he suddenly announced, "I was thinking of asking Kath to look after the shop for a few days so that we can head over to Bermagui for a break. What do you think?" Both Mum, who was cashing up the till at the end of the day, and I froze in amazement. Dad never takes time off. My mind was too muddled to reply and even Mum was lost for words, which for a Greek woman is virtually unheard of!

"There's a long weekend coming up," he continued, "and if we pack the van up on, say, Wednesday night, then we can get an early start the next day and be there by lunchtime. So, what do you think?" He reached over and placed his hand on Mum's arm and squeezed it gently. "I think we all deserve a break, don't you?" Another brief silence ensued. "And you could bring your surf board with you." This comment was obviously directed at me, because the image of Mum on a surfboard is not one for the faint-hearted.

"Kath, she a very good woman," Mum agreed. Then she looked over at me. I looked from Dad to her and back again.

"Really, Dad? Do I have to come? I don't really feel up to a long journey."

"It's been a tough time for us all, Tel, but if you're going to be working all through summer, then this might be the only chance we can have a family holiday together. Maybe our journey across the mountains to the sea will be a journey worthy of Odysseus himself." His eyes fairly sparkled with anticipation. "Whatever happened to your adventurous spirit?"

"OK, Dad," I said, smiling at his ability to always weave Odysseus into nearly every story he told. "I'm in."

The owl and
the pussycat
went to sea

KATH DONNELLY WAS a big lady with an even bigger heart. She might have moved slowly, she might have had a bad back and she might have smoked like a chimney, but Kath was a beautiful lady in the best possible way – she loved everyone. And not only that, she was as honest as the days are long. She used to baby sit me when I was little, when Mum couldn't afford to be away from the shop for long, so I kind of grew up with her always being there. She was the one who called the ambulance when Chook decked me – though what she was doing in Kev's cement works is a mystery to me. It's a well-known fact that Kev hates smoking, hates people who use magic words and definitely doesn't like big sheilas. But for some reason, in Kev's famous book of rules, Kath is an exception.

She knew our shop from inside out having helped out on a myriad of occasions. "I've got a soft spot for Greeks," she'd say. "Must be because most of them look like Antony Quinn". She'd chuckle her raspy chuckle and tap grey ash from her cigarette into her little mobile ashtray with its silvered lid, before clicking it shut and popping it back in her voluminous handbag. She wasn't the fastest worker but despite her intimidating size, Kath could keep going from dawn to dusk.

She appeared at 5.15 on the dot on Thursday morning, just as Dad slammed the rear door of the van shut. "Thanks, Kath," we all said in unison, before each of us in turn was pulled into her ample bosom for a farewell hug. She wiped away the tears with a small lace handkerchief while rummaging through her handbag for her packet of ciggies. Kath cried at the drop of a hat, which usually called for another round of reassuring cuddles. Small clouds of talc wafted from various parts of her clothing. Then it was time to leave.

The bench seat up the front allowed plenty of room for the three of us. Tucked behind the front seat was enough food for a whole team of footy players!

"Have you got your medications with you, Telemachus?" Dad asked as he backed into the driver's seat of the van.

"They're in my kit bag," I replied, indicating the back of the van where the camping equipment, fishing gear, all

Mum's cooking gear and my surfboard were settling into each other's company. Mum didn't like to think of anyone going hungry so to the untrained eye it appeared she'd brought half the contents of her kitchen with her.

The road through Wyallum to Kooranoomah is good at that time of day so we scooted along through the pretty countryside at a healthy lick. But once we headed up into the hills, things got really interesting.

We'd decided to go the straight route, which takes you through Kosciuszko National Park. There's no doubt that it's a beautiful area of the world, but there's not much else up there besides good old Mother Nature as far as the eye can see. The road twists and turns like a mallee root on a bad hair day. Poor old Mum doesn't travel too well at the best of times, so we had to stop regularly for her to get some fresh air. I don't think the smell of onions and fresh cauliflower would've helped her much.

After we'd hit the high country I left Mum and Dad in the front and made a nest for myself amongst the sleeping bags, pillows and beach towels, and managed to miss most of the trip from Cooma to Bermagui.

When I eventually woke up, the first thing I heard was the surf pounding on the small beach close by the camp site. It's one of those magnetic sounds that just draws you to its source. I wandered down to the beach and stood there with the waves lapping at my feet, soaking it all in like a balm for my bruised soul. The breeze coming in off the ocean softly massaged my face, played with my hair and made me feel like a little kid again. I sucked in a huge lungful of air, stretched my arms wide and screamed out, "Yeeeeeessss!" at the top of my voice. The air, the sea and the heavens above took that sound and carried it to some secret place where, perhaps, some unseen spirit heard it and smiled.

I studied the waves for some time trying to work out where the break was and which area would be the best for me to go surfing. There was not another person in sight. This was going to be amazing! Finally I turned my attention to the top end of the beach. The camp site was visible from where I was and I could see Dad getting our stuff organised while Mum checked her provisions to make sure nothing had spilled or broken. I could see them moving but the only sound came from the sea behind me. I knew I should really be helping them, but I was trying to work out how short I'd get if I stayed there for much longer, as I slowly sank into the sand with the water creating whirlpools around my ankles.

A seagull flew low over me and squawked loudly. I ducked involuntarily. "Mad bastard!" I shouted up at it as it lazily flew off to the far end of the beach. Just as it disappeared, I noticed a track through the bush that appeared to lead to what I assumed must be the next beach along. I whistled up at Dad and his head jerked up as if he'd been stung. I gesticulated to him that I was just going to explore a bit. From the semaphores he sent back I worked out that he seemed pretty happy with the idea.

I wandered down the beach taking childish delight in seeing my footprints vanishing as the surf surged up the beach behind me. Was life like that, I wondered? Do we leave footprints behind us that just get washed away in time? It was a bleak thought that I batted away like an annoying bush fly. There was no way the world would forget Telemachus Alysandratos!

I reached the track and followed it over a limestone ridge covered with scrubby bushes. I clambered over a low ridge and on the other side was a ripper of a little beach, its high tide mark spotted with seashells and the occasional piece of sea-sculpted wood. The beach was about fifty metres long and wouldn't be any good for surfing, but high above the waterline at the far end of the beach was what looked to my eyes like a cave! Now that would be worth exploring! There was no time to do it now as I knew I should get back to camp and help out. But if the weather held, then tomorrow should prove to be a very interesting day indeed.

A god on my side

EVEN THOUGH I'D slept in the back of the van for most of the way, that night I slept for Australia! I vaguely remembered listening to the hypnotic dumping of small waves on the beach and hearing the soft shrill sound of shells being washed back and forth by the ocean. I smiled when, on the abyss of sleep, I heard the sound of an owl calling in the woods where we'd made camp. That night I had a beautiful dream about the Irish nurse who'd been kind to me in hospital. But in my dream she was dressed like one of those ancient Greek goddesses and looked a real stunner!

Something jolted me awake early in the morning but as my dream rapidly dissolved, I made a mental note for when I got back to find out how long the Irish nurse was going to be working at the hospital for, and what the best way to contact her was. But deep down I knew that I'd chicken out.

The soft pinks of the dawn sunrise were not a bad compensation for being awake so early. Even the native birds were raucous in their desire to get me out of my sleeping bag and embrace the new day. Mum and Dad had cleared a sleeping area for themselves in the back of the van, and it remained still and quiet at that hour. Slipping on a singlet and struggling into my old boardies, I muttered to myself, "Time for a quick exploration." My belly wobbled, which was a tad disconcerting, but it hardened my resolve to see this holiday as the first step in regaining my normal svelte self. My plan was to jog along the beach and have a look at the cave that I'd seen the day before.

Just before I slipped away, my conscience reared up and prodded me. I'd better leave a note for Mum and Dad. One thing I'd learned from the seeming eternity of chaos popularly known as the teenage years was to keep the parents onside. I searched around until I found the Special K cereal packet, then tore off the top, pulled a pencil out of my rucksack and scribbled a note to let them know where I'd gone. It only took a minute but that surely saved me days of recriminations if I hadn't done so!

Conscience salved, I set out.

By the time I'd reached the limestone ridge, I was panting pretty hard. It appeared that it was going to take more than a gentle jog to get me back into condition.

I stood there and took it all in.

The world looked so damned beautiful at that time of day. It was magical: the early light, the freshness in the air, the beach, the ocean … everything combined to lift the spirits and make me believe that anything was possible – even the impossible.

I continued jogging across the beach and scrambled up to the mouth of the cave with my lungs threatening to burst into fire. My stomach chose that moment to remind me that I hadn't brought any food with me and it also came to me that I'd forgotten to take my morning meds. Maybe it was that, or maybe it was all the running that had made me feel light-headed. I sat down just inside the cave and gazed over the waves. Then I heard that owl again.

I must have dozed off because when I opened my eyes I found myself staring at the ceiling of the cave from a supine position. Then I heard a voice calling. It was an accented voice, but an accent with which I was pretty familiar. It appeared that some guy was calling for his dog. I got up and stepped into the morning sunlight. The light blinded me as the image of a young man, not much older than me, came into focus right in front of me.

"Whose shepherd are you?" he asked, while looking around in all directions for signs of his dog.

"Huh?" I replied. "I'm here on…" Before I could fully answer, he darted off, calling back over his shoulder that he'd return in a moment. Then I heard him shouting, "Argos, come here boy. Come on Argos." I lost sight of him. My foggy brain couldn't quite wrap itself around those past few seconds. Someone's shepherd? I distractedly looked around the cave, not really seeing what I was looking at. It was a large space, clean and dry and obviously well used by someone as there were lots of different footprints in the dirt. I was just going to head over to a pile of what looked like fishing nets when my new friend arrived. Behind him trotted an old dog. The beast had soft rheumy eyes and yellow teeth. It ambled over to me and gave be the big 'sniff over' – checking out my crotch and backside with particular attention! What is it with dogs?

"Argos is my father's dog," the youth said, squatting down and gently tousling the hound's head behind its ears. "He may be old, but what he lacks in youth he makes up for with wisdom. If he didn't like you he'd probably rip your throat out," he added casually.

"Nice dog," I said, and joined in rubbing Argos' head as if to cement our burgeoning relationship. "My name's Telemachus," I said, offering my hand to Argos's young master.

He glanced at me with wonder in his eyes. "So is mine!" he said. "Are you from Ithaca?" he asked, his eyes narrowing. "Because I've never met anyone on this island with the same name before. And believe me, I know everyone!"

"No," I replied, although the word 'Ithaca' did stir some confusion in my already muddled mind. "I'm from Yarramah!"

"Have you travelled far?" he asked, his baffled expression no doubt mirroring my own. He settled back onto his haunches and began to draw idly in the dirt with a stick. Argos meanwhile had retreated to the edge of the cave where he slumped to the floor, resting his long, hairy snout on his paws.

"Yeah, it's a fair way from here. So where's Ithaca?" It seemed a reasonable question but stirred a strange response from my new friend.

"This is Ithaca, my friend," he said, spreading his arms wide. "I am Telemachus, son of Odysseus, lord of the island of Ithaca. My father has been gone these last twenty years and we grieve for his absence. My mother is besieged by suitors who want to take our lands and our possessions. They mock me. There are too many of them and I lack my father's guile to defeat them." He paused, and as if talking to himself added, "but the gods are on my side. Athene will never desert my father. Always has she been on the side of righteousness. She will come to my aid."

"Wow." The words escaped my lips before my mind could catch up with what Telemachus had said. "My dad used to tell me about Ithaca and about Odysseus, the war at Troy, and I loved the bit about Calypso – I wouldn't mind getting that lucky," I smirked to myself. "So you've read the book as well, have you?" I asked in all innocence.

Telemachus looked blankly at me. "Book? What book? Tell me about this thing you call a book! Didn't you hear me? My father is lost and I need to find him before it's too late." He looked at me strangely. "Are you mad? Have the gods turned your brain to mush?"

"Strange you should say that, friend, because you took the words right out of my mouth!" We stared at each other, both our minds struggling with the same question: "Who are you?"

"Take me to your house," I challenged him. The sound of the sea rolling onto the sand filled the short silence.

"Come," he said to Argos, slapping his thigh. He flashed me a look, daring me to follow.

When we left the cave we climbed up a steep path cut into the cliff face above its opening. When we reached the top, it looked like the land had been cleared for some distance as there were white sheep dotted around the visible countryside. There were even some small olive groves and some of the trees looked seriously old and gnarled. As we walked on, we passed a low stone hut with a freshly thatched roof – it must be some heritage thingy, I thought. But it wouldn't be much cop if there were a bushfire around here. I was surprised the country fire authority had let that pass!

As we approached a small settlement I began to get a queasy feeling in my stomach. It was slowly dawning on me that there was something really not quite right with what I was seeing. I was at the point of thinking that I should turn around straight away and head back to the camp site when, in a flash, Argos was by my side nuzzling into me and almost pushing me forward. I crouched down next to him and ruffled his coat, which caused him to fall on the ground and expose his ageing genitals – what is it with dogs?

"What's going on, Argos?" I muttered to him, rubbing his chest and getting an ecstatic growl in return. "Where am, I old fella?" Wild thyme grew where the old hound lay wriggling on the ground and the air was filled with its pungent perfume. The friendship of the dog and the scent of the crushed herbs had a calming effect on my senses, so, letting out a big sigh, my shoulders relaxed and I said to myself, "I can do this."

We had walked some distance when we arrived at a walled household. There were other buildings nearby but none really as grand as this one. I had come to the conclusion that I was having one of those vivid dreams that the specialist had warned me about that I might have with my meds. I'd already had a few, but only those ones where you're trying to walk through mud or where you're shouting at someone but only a tiny sound comes out of your mouth.

This one was fun!

"Come in and take some refreshment," my new friend said. Once he had set foot through the guarded doorway, everything seemed to change. For a start, it was much cooler inside those walls. The courtyard was shaded by an old olive tree and a fountain whispered magically as cool water cascaded from its sculptured summit. On either side of the tree, there were wooden tables showing signs of a recently eaten meal, with two servants brushing the debris from the flagstones beneath.

But the biggest change was in Telemachus himself. He began to act all hoity-toity, shouting at the guys and telling them to bring fresh wine and dainties! This had to be a dream because no-one speaks like that unless they're a bit arty-farty. I couldn't wait to tell Kev about this when I woke up!

"Wait here," he commanded me.

"OK, mate," I replied, holding my hand up to deflect his toffiness. "Keep your hair on! Argos and I are quite happy where we are, aren't we boy?" I turned to the dog and scratched him between his ears, which resulted in the standard canine response!

"I need to inform my mother of your arrival," he said more reasonably.

"Go ahead, mate," I answered. "I'll wait with Argos." Argos was loving this!

Sitting in the quiet courtyard with just the healing sounds of the fountain and the dog's gently panting breath, I got a moment to try and analyse what was going on using the limited brain power I had. To my way of thinking, it looked as if the stories Dad had told me of Odysseus had been stored somewhere in my head and that the medication had flicked a switch resulting in this incredibly vivid dream. Maybe this epilepsy thing had an upside after all!

"Argos," I said, "that's disgusting." I waved away the fetid smell that was coming from his direction. If a dog could smile, then I'd say that right then Argos definitely smiled!

That dog knew more than he was letting on. Once the smell had departed I leaned down and ruffled his old mop once more, saying, "You're a clever boy, aren't you?"

"He is, indeed," came a beautiful voice from the shaded area of a doorway which led into the house. The beauty of her voice was matched by her physical beauty. This had to be Penelope, the wife of Odysseus. Dad had a thing for her when he was reading the *Iliad* to me as a kid. Now I knew why!

"Telemachus has been telling me all about you, Telemachus." A small grin lifted one corner of her mouth. She stepped out into the dappled sunlight which only seemed to accentuate her beauty. What made her appear even more magical, at least to my eyes, was that her face had the faintest of lines as if she'd been touched by some ancient wisdom.

Normally when we Aussies meet someone for the first time, we say something like 'G'day', but intuitively that didn't feel right. I drew myself up to my full height, inclined my head and simply said, "Telemachus Alysandratos, my lady."

The grin I had noted earlier now reached up to embrace her eyes. "Come, Telemachus, sit by my side in the shade and tell me your story. You are a stranger and may have word of my husband Odysseus who has been gone these many years. Strangers are uncommon in these troubled times. Come, sit here," and she patted the chair that had miraculously appeared next to hers. The service in this place was definitely five star!

"To be quite honest, my lady, I really don't know where to begin." I furiously scratched my scalp in search of a beginning. "If you want to know, then I reckon that this is all just a dream. I shouldn't be here, but I am! It all feels so weird and at the same time it all feels quite normal. Sorry," I said, "if what I am saying seems a load of rubbish, but I'm just a kid from the country who's recently been told he's got epilepsy." I looked across at Penelope. Her motherly eyes held nothing but gentle empathy, so I stumbled on. "It's pretty embarrassing, really. What it means is that for no reason I suddenly fall down, then I thrash around on the ground and I bite my tongue. But the worst of it is that I wet my pants, too." I studied her face for any signs of insight or judgement. What I got was the gentle pressure of her soft hand on mine.

"The gods often choose unexpected people to give their gifts to, my son," she said. "You must be a very special person." I looked for traces of humour in her face, half expecting that she was pulling my leg, but none appeared. She really meant what she was saying.

"Forgive my rudeness, my lady," I mumbled, "but it sure doesn't feel like a gift." The smile that wreathed her face was almost beatific, and then she laughed. It was such a light, soft laugh, like the sound I'd imagine fairy bells would make in the gentlest of breezes.

"Oh, Telemachus. Greatness isn't easy, just as suffering isn't easy, but both are inextricably intertwined." Then she said the strangest of things: "Did you hear the owl call?"

I'd seen old folk sitting on park benches with their mouths wide open before, and often thought they looked pretty stupid. Now here I was with my jaw fairly sitting on my chest.

"Athene," she said. "Long has she been the protector of Odysseus. She has brought you here for a purpose. If she is behind this then expect the unexpected." She squeezed my hand a little tighter. "But where are my manners? You must be hungry." She called for servants to bring fruit and wine to refresh me and sent others off to prepare a bath for me. "I must return to my room," she continued, "before the suitors return. They are the bane of my life until my husband returns. Yet now you are here, for some reason my heart feels lighter." She pointed to the refreshments that were set on the table in front of me. "Eat and rest, and then we will talk more later."

At this point, Telemachus reappeared, looking grumpier than ever. "Why will no-one listen to me?" he moaned, hitting his clenched fist against a pillar. "Am I not the son of the great Odysseus?" he said, every word dripping with sarcasm. "And even though the great man has been gone these twenty years, I'm still ignored! What do I have to do to get the people to respect me?"

I couldn't stop myself. "Hey, Tel, you need to take a chill pill. Being the top dog is a tough job. I wouldn't rush into taking it on before you're ready."

Telemachus stared at me and I could sense a rage building inside of him. Dad says I have one of those infectious grins, which has got me out of a lot of sticky situations over the years, but this time it didn't seem to be working. Telemachus stepped before me. As if on cue, Argos appeared, rolled on his back and exposed his wrinkled genitals to one and all. Talk about an icebreaker. That dog has instincts that are superhuman! Both of us burst out laughing and the other Telemachus reverted to the nice guy that I'd met earlier.

"Let's eat," he said. "I'm hungry."

After some minutes of silent feasting, I noticed just how much food two hungry young guys can pack away when their mothers aren't watching. Amazing amounts!

Telemachus spoke. "We're going to have to think about what to call you. Having two Telemachuses in one house is going to cause complications." He lifted his face archly before adding, "and it's my house." I liked this guy.

"Well, at college they call me all sorts of things, some of them even quite nice actually, but the usual one is 'wog'."

"Hmm," Telemachus intoned. "What is a college?" The question caught me off balance. Most folk seem to be more concerned about the word 'wog' – not that it worries me too much. The Irish are called 'paddies', the English are called

'Pommy bastards' and the Italians are called 'wops'. Most of us are pretty happy with those monikers. I suppose it's how you take it. There are some who get really upset with the whole name calling thing. For instance, I'd never use the words 'nigger' or 'slope', because to me, they're more like weapons than epithets. And everyone knows that 'Pommy bastard' is a term of endearment – it's only an attack weapon when you say 'whingeing Pom', then it's on for young and old! In the end it's just laziness: not being bothered to remember someone's name and going for the easy option. But most people grow out of it eventually.

"It's where they round up all the young people for eight hours a day and pretend to teach them stuff. Mainly it's just to keep the kids off the streets and out of their mum's hair! It works for some, but most of us would prefer to go fishing or surfing."

I could see the thought forming in his mind about surfing, but he stopped himself.

"What about Alexander?"

"As a name? For me? Yep. That's fine," I agreed. "At college some of the kids call me Alex, but Alexander's good." What's in a name? I thought to myself. Especially when it's all happening in a dream. I must remember to ask my specialist about these medications. Geez – I hope they don't give me any nightmares!

"I need to see my grandfather today, Alexander," he said. "I am troubled by how bold the suitors have become." I could see his rage bubble up again as he spoke. "They are eating us out of house and home. It's only Mother's guile that is keeping them from seizing her as a trophy, too." I tried to remember how she did that but decided that perhaps I'd leave that conversation for another dream!

"Where does Pops live?" I asked in innocence.

"Pops?" he fired back at me. "In Ithaca we hold our grandparents in high esteem. Laertes is a great man who has been much reduced since my father Odysseus left for the war in Troy. It's been even harder since his wife Anticlea died of grief at losing her son." He took a breath, and carried on more calmly. "My grandfather lives on a small farm not far from here. He loves his land. He will be pleased to see us. Come. We leave now."

"Hold on," I interjected, reaching for a luscious bunch of grapes to take with me, "I'm a hungry lad and need my food!" Telemachus smiled in return as he plucked the juiciest one from the bunch and popped it in his mouth.

"Me, too," he said.

We walked in silence out from the village and through the dusty countryside until we saw a small homestead in the fields below. It was surrounded by well-husbanded fields, which were dotted with white sheep grazing amongst the olive trees and vines.

Laertes was tending his vines as we approached. "What do you want?" he grumped while carrying on with his work. So much for being pleased to see us!

Without missing a beat, Telemachus said, "Greetings, grandfather. I bring my mother's blessings to your house."

"Hmm," was the succinct response.

"I also bring my friend Telemachus Alysandratos of Yarramah to meet you. He has travelled a great distance to get here. I thought you may like to meet him." Laertes turned briefly and looked me up and down.

"Stranger, eh? Never heard of Yarramah. Maybe you are Assyrian?" He spat in the dirt at my feet which, I suppose, summed up his attitude towards Assyria! I thought of telling him where I was from but decided to skip the idea, for obvious reasons.

"Greetings, Laertes," I began. "I bring you greetings from my family." I thought it sounded quite a good reply.

He stabbed his hoe into the ground and leaned on the handle. "Why is it that whenever my family has a problem to solve they come and see me, and the rest of the time they treat me as if I don't exist?"

Telemachus looked stunned. "But, grandfather," he began.

Laertes cut him short. Adopting a more conciliatory approach he proceeded. "It's not all your fault, Telemachus, although you don't come as often as you used to." He wiped his brow. "An old man can only expect one thing: to get older. You young people have one common flaw. You think that you're going to live forever, but unfortunately the gods decree that it doesn't work that way. And as you get older you become acutely aware of that." Resting his gnarled and arthritic hand on his grandson's shoulder, he finished, "I'm running out of time, my son. Odysseus has been gone for so long and the wound of his absence still bites deep into my heart. It killed dear Anticlea." Tears welled in his old eyes. He looked off into the distance but saw nothing.

"I'm sorry, grandfather," Telemachus said quietly. "I'll try to be a better grandson in the future."

I felt moved by what the old man was saying. It struck a chord in my own heart. Those who love us the most are the very ones we take for granted – Laertes had just told me that. In fact, there were so many old people around the town who carried an air of forlorn longing with them: now I understood why that was.

"How's that old dog, Argos?" Laertes asked while giving a big sniff. "Is he still running the place since my son left?" Although there was humour in his voice, I could sense that Telemachus didn't get the joke.

"Why does no-one believe that I can rule in my father's stead? Everyone treats me like a child who still suckles at his mother's breast." Suddenly the tension in this family situation had sky-rocketed.

"I know how you feel," I interrupted. "Back in Yarramah I'm treated as a kid, mainly because most of the time I act like one!" I thought that sounded funny, but no-one was laughing. "Mind you, it's been worse since I got epilepsy."

The tense silence continued. "You know, it's where you fall to the floor and shake like a lunatic," I added, giving a graphic demonstration of the shaking part.

That must have impressed them because their eyes opened wide and I could clearly see that Laertes definitely needed some dental work – his teeth were awful! I thought their response a little strange because whenever it came up back home, most people shuffled around and mumbled something like, "Sorry about that, Tel," or even just, "Oh!"

"Did you hear an owl?" Telemachus asked in an awed tone.

"What is this with the owl?" I asked. "If you must know, I did! So what?"

Grandfather and grandson looked at one another and smiled in that annoying way which suggested that they knew something that I didn't. "What?" I demanded.

It was Laertes who spoke. "Few there are who are blessed by the gods," he began.

"If you think epilepsy is a blessing, I can sincerely assure you that it's a bastard of a condition. Sorry," I immediately corrected myself, imagining that Mum could hear everything I was saying.

"I believe you, Telemachus," he continued, "but with all great blessings come great burdens, too, and hidden in the darkness of most wounds there is always a spark of great beauty." He looked me fair square in the eyes and I saw in his eyes great wisdom mixed with great sadness and suffering. "But come in out of the sun and take some refreshments. I may live simply but my wine and olives are the best to be found on the island. Are you coming, too?" he asked his grandson. Telemachus looked uncomfortable

"Forgive me grandfather, but I will remain outside. You have not visited our home since my father, your son, left for the wars this twenty years past. I think it would not befit our understanding to change the arrangements at this time." Glancing at me, he said, "I will wait out here for you, Alexander."

A flicker of confusion crossed the old man's face, and then you could almost hear the proverbial penny drop.

It was dark inside the old man's hut and very basic – and I mean *really* basic: a table and chair by the only window, and what appeared to be a camp bed covered in some sort of animal skins that had obviously seen better days. Thank goodness the window was just an empty space otherwise the smell would have been overpowering. It reminded me of some of the bachelor farmers who lived way out in the bush where we deliver extras if they get sick. Old man smells.

"Do you get many visitors?" I asked absentmindedly.

"What do you think?" came the curt reply. "Mentor is the only one who comes here. He is of my generation and sees beyond the wild passions of youth. He, too, remembers the past. But now, like us few aged ones, he is also too feeble to prevent it happening all over again – anger, resentment, greed, jealously, deceit and worst of all, war."

To say that it put a cloud over the conversation would be putting it mildly.

"Tell me more about the owl."

Laertes had found a stone jug concealed in a dark cool place and poured its golden contents into a plain goblet. Officially I had 'never' drunk alcohol but as a Greek teenager who liked to party maybe I had tasted it before, but nothing like this. It was like honey, except it was so light; it was so cool and left my tongue feeling like it had been touched by the dew of a cold spring morning. But mostly it sent a glorious warmth all through me. "This is good," I said grinning widely.

My host raised a wrinkled smile on his sad old face. "The nectar of the gods," he said. He savoured a small sip from his own goblet and placed it back on the table. When he looked through the empty window I could see a deep tiredness etched into his features. His silvered hair may have thinned at the back, yet over his ears it hung down in lanky tresses. He brushed it back out of his eyes and just stared at the view for some minutes. I took another draft of my wine – "Really good!" I thought to myself as I began to detect a faint buzzing in my head. "Yep, this is really, really good!"

"When Odysseus was a child like you, we'd travel far around this island planting trees and husbanding our flocks. I taught him all I knew. But the gods had other plans for him. Athene had watched him grow and knew the power of the man, but she also knew the great goodness that dwelt in his heart. Perhaps that is why she has protected him from harm over all the years. But she hasn't prevented him from hurt and suffering. These twenty years apart from his wife and family – his father too – would be a source of deep pain for him."

He poured me some more wine. I took another draft.

Placing his arm on my shoulder, he said, "Athene comes to those whom she seeks to befriend and oft times her voice is likened to that of an owl."

I was not sure whether it was the wine or what Laertes was trying to tell me that had made my head start to feel very dizzy. Perhaps it was both, but before I could muster my thoughts, the sound of people talking outside the door interrupted us.

"Mentor!" Laertes said with a slight grin. "That man can smell my wine as a wolf smells a sheep." He stood up and went out to greet his friend. I followed, knocking my stool over as I went.

After the low light inside the hut, the bright sunshine temporarily blinded me. All I could see were two black figures before me. One of them was the familiar outline of Telemachus, yet the other looked vaguely familiar too. As my eyes slowly adjusted, and just as Laertes was introducing me, Mentor's face came into view.

"Geez," I gasped. "I don't believe it."

Kate and Frank

THE SERRIED SURFACE of the sea glistened with the light of a million diamonds. The sucking sounds of the surf caressing the sand had a soothing effect on my soul. It was the day after my dream and I'd just had a really good surf. I walked up the beach and plonked myself down next to Dad. He was in his element sitting there in his favourite Hawaiian shirt with his straw trilby holiday hat perched on his semi-balding head – no customers, no delivery deadlines, no bills to pay; for him this was almost as good as paradise.

There is something incredibly bonding about sitting on the beach with your old man and just staring at the ocean. The sounds, the sky, the sights, the smells, they all infuse your senses and murmur a special language which only your heart can understand. After a while I began to tell him about the dream. He listened patiently as I recalled all I could remember – which, as it turned out, was quite a lot. When it came to telling him about Mentor, he seemed surprised at first, but then I saw the beginnings of a smirk start to reshape his lips.

"Kevin O'Ryan, you say. Hmm," he intoned to himself. He tossed a small pebble toward the receding water. "He's an amazing man, Kev. Most people just take him for a tough guy and a larrikin but I've never had any problems with him. But the women," and this time his grin won hands down, "the women, either they love him or they hate him." He smoothed out an area of sand and patted it gently flat. He poked a couple of holes for eyes before drawing a face. He smoothed it over, patting it flat again. "You know why they call him Rooster, don't you?"

I looked sideways at him, my grin reflecting his. It's always a bit uncomfortable when your own dad says suggestive things, but maybe he was just beginning to accept me as a man. "Yeah," I answered, "I hear he's a bit of a goer," before resuming my gaze at a new set of breakers casually rolling in from the ocean.

Another languid pause ensued. The waves broke on the beach and the air was filled with the soothing sound of shifting sand as the ocean receded once more.

"You know what, Tel? It doesn't surprise me that you mixed up Kev and Mentor in your dreams. They have a great deal in common. You should get Kev to tell you about

Chook when you get back," Dad said. "It's an interesting story and tells you a lot about both of them." Knowing Dad, and by the tone he used, I knew that was all he was going to tell me.

I can still picture that weekend. But it went all too quickly, hastened on by the fact that for some reason my meds weren't working as well as they should. I started having what the French delightfully call 'absences'.

To the casual observer, it looked like I'd just stopped paying attention and was staring off into the distance. It'd only last a few seconds, and at first I managed to cover it up. Then one of them lasted a bit longer and it really put the wind up Mum.

"We go home," she declared emphatically, and there was no way anyone was going to disagree!

The funny thing about those petit mal episodes (which was the official name for them according to Doc) was that I had no recollection of them. I seemed to remember hearing Mum speaking but I had no idea what she was saying, if indeed it was her, and afterwards I felt 'different'. It's difficult to describe. I suppose it's like any dream that you have, and the way they dissolve into the mists of your forgettery during the process of waking up! Yet they both leave a lingering trace, like the memory of perfume.

"We can either increase the dose of your current medication or stay on the same dose and add in one of the newer tablets." Mum looked from Doc Buckley to me and then back to the good doctor.

"It fix him?" she asked.

The dear man seemed to struggle at the wide rift between medicine as a science and medicine as an art. He toyed with his half-moon glasses as if trying to shape a simple answer out of them. "I wouldn't be suggesting a new treatment, Mrs Alysandratos, if I didn't think it was going to help." He paused, and I reflected that doctors must be taught that melodramatic pause at med school – the one that comes just before they deliver the bad news. "However," – I knew it! – "there are no guarantees and there is always the possibility of some unwanted side effects." Having delivered this double-edged piece of information, he assumed his 'you can trust me, I'm a doctor' look.

"What is this unwanted business?" she shot back at him. "Telemachus, he my son. You make better, not worse. You proper doctor, eh?"

It seemed to me that this conversation was heading in a direction which wasn't going to help anyone, so I interrupted her. "Mum, I think Doc is trying to say that he has to do something to stop these mini fits. My understanding is that he thinks that taking another type of tablet will help. But it's like buying a tray of fresh apricots – you can't guarantee that all of them are going to be perfectly ripe."

"Ha," she beamed. "My son explain everything. Why you not tell me that?" she accused the doc. He attempted a smile but failed miserably.

"I'll see him in four weeks to see how he's going. By the way, Tel, how's study going?" The simple answer was that it wasn't! Between feeling cut off from my friends because of all the things I wasn't allowed to do and the medication making me feel more dopey than usual, the challenge of studying for school had slipped well down my list of things to do.

"Fine, thanks Doc," I replied automatically. By then Doc Buckley had already buried his head in the pile of paperwork in front of him.

"Good to hear," he replied, briefly lifting his head with an expression which said 'and please close the door after you'.

He was a busy man! And believe me, I was relieved that he didn't pursue that particular line of interrogation. The school had been really good about everything. I didn't have any major examinations until my final high school ones the following year, so it was assumed that I'd soon catch up once I'd got over 'it'. Apparently, I was a good student!

We took the prescription to the local pharmacy and handed it over the counter. Sheryl, the assistant in Mr Bonner's pharmacy, had worked there for some years and knew more about the customers than he did, and probably more about the medications she was required to issue than he did, too. She was whip-smart and whip-thin and possessed the heart of an angel. So when she looked at the prescription and then looked at me with what I can only describe as eyes full of pity, my heart sank.

"It fix my son?" my mother asked.

Sheryl flicked her blue eyes in Mum's direction. "He needs to take them twice a day. Make sure he does." There was genuine kindness behind her professional, pixie-like features, but I'd seen what I'd seen in that brief glance: an expression which appeared to confirm that I wasn't exactly facing a bright and glittering future! Yet somehow I felt she understood what I was going through. Suffering can do things like that. She disappeared into the next room where Mr Bonner performed his alchemy.

"I go help your father in the shop," Mum said. "I settle up later, OK?"

I was left alone to shuffle around the shop, peering at hot water bottles and nappy pins, medicines for the relief of flatulence and packets of aspirin which appeared to be able to treat anything. A few minutes later, the two of them reappeared.

"Hi, Tel. Good to see you," Mr Bonner said in his unfailingly affable way. He was slightly tubby and slightly balding, yet there was nothing slight about his intelligence. He even looked like an owl when he peered through his thick, round glasses. "Sorry to hear about the epilepsy thing. Pain in the backside, eh?" He glanced at me as if assessing how well I was coping. "Mmm," he purred. "Now with this new medication it is important that you take it as directed and that you don't miss any tablets. You also need to carry on with the other one Dr Buckley gave you."

"Sure thing, Mr Bonner," I replied in an automatic fashion, though not really focusing on what he was saying.

He came around to my side of the counter. "Ever heard of Socrates? St Theresa of Avila?"

This sounded like one of those new TV quizzes. "Socrates – yes. St Theresa? Hey, I'm Greek, Mr Bonner," I replied with a wry smile.

"OK, smartypants." Mr Bonner may be the pharmacist but he had an easy sense of humour. "Have you ever seen the TV series *Wagon Trail*? Remember Seth Adams, the Trail Master? He was played by an actor called Ward Bond. Back in the day, he used to be in a lot of films with John Wayne. Guess what? That cowboy Bond had epilepsy too, just like Socrates and St Theresa. Dostoyevsky was another." Seeing the blank look on my face he added, "He was a famous Russian writer from last century, though he's not really my cup of tea!"

He placed his arm around my shoulder. "Tel, I'm not saying that this epilepsy thing is going to make your life any easier, but don't let it stop you becoming the great man you can be. Don't let it be an excuse to give up. I've watched you since you were this high," and he indicated an area just above his knee, "and I know what a fine young man you are and what wonderful parents you have, too." The gentle pressure he applied to my shoulder reached my heart.

"Thanks, Mr Bonner. I appreciate that."

The harsh reality was that the new combination of medications was harder to get used to than I thought. Talk about being tired after sleeping for ten hours straight! I reckon I could have slept for Australia. But I adjusted to it: not that I had much choice in the matter.

Time flowed on in a foggy sort of way. In the last few weeks of school I took to taking a stroll up to the end of Lisle Street just to hang out at Kev's place. He was a man of few words when he was working, but give him a beer and he'd talk the legs off a donkey!

There was something strangely reassuring about the sight of a man working his guts out just to make an honest quid and never complain one iota about it. Not that the taxman would probably agree with me on that! Even his little transistor radio in its faux brown leather case seemed so ... solid and reliable.

From time to time, someone would meander in and give him the regulation, "G'day Kev," then wait for him to finish what he was doing. If someone interrupted him while he was busy, the air temperature would drop 50 degrees in a second. Kev could be one tough bastard!

Eventually, school finished and I began my holiday job with him at the cement works. I began at 7 am each day from Monday to Friday, and worked through until six each evening. Mind you, Kev was always there before me with his tranny playing music in the background, and the cement mixer churning away on the other side of the large shed. If

I had to describe his attitude towards his wet-behind-the-ears employee, it would be cruel but fair. If nothing else, during my time working for him, I began to appreciate the value of hard work. Even the repetitive nature of the work came to be strangely calming – almost meditative. Needless to say, all of our labours were soaked in sweat.

Each morning Kev would greet me with "G'day, Tel. You taken your meds?" For such a testosterone-driven guy, he had a heart of gold.

The days in the cement works were long, but not without the occasional, and always interesting, interruption by one of the local 'cockies'. Such interruption nearly always resulted in Kev and me heading out to their properties way out in the back blocks, in order to size up their particular needs.

We'd head out in his old Ford F100 ute with a load of Kev's fence posts in the back and five litres of water in the front. "Just in case the radiator gets thirsty. The beer's behind the seat in the Esky." he'd say … and he wasn't joking. Kev and beer were like bacon and eggs, Astaire and Rogers, Romeo and Juliet – inseparable!

I'd sit in the passenger seat feeling, like a young lord as we bounced down dusty tracks, casting a professional eye over burnt brown paddocks and flocks of straggly brown sheep. Each paddock had its own dam to catch the infrequent rains. At this time of year the dams were often just muddy hollows, pock-marked by animal footprints. Some of the dams had battered windmills to pump up the water hidden below the arid surface, yet in the windless air of early summer they stood silent and still, adding to the feeling of isolation in this harsh landscape.

Out in the bush, out on those vast plains, the world is inhabited by a different sort of folk.

One particular day, Kev informed me that we were headed to Miss O'Driscoll's place. "If you call her Mrs, you probably won't make it back alive to the truck," Kev shouted to me over the noise of the engine, before pulling up at a freshly painted weatherboard cottage. The building was surrounded by a trimmed hedge which protected a mini oasis containing roses, hollyhocks and a tiny patch of grass! In the middle of the grass stood the only tree to be seen for fifty kilometres and which gave a cool, dappled light to the garden nestled at its feet. In the all-pervading, torrid heat, that single tree had the magical effect of soothing the mind and relaxing the body.

"Nice place," I said as we stepped up onto the open wooden verandah.

"Don't forget to clean your boots before you go in. Miss O'Driscoll's a real toff: doesn't appreciate dirt on her carpets." He blinked like an owl before adding, "But she's a good sort." Then finally, "And don't stare at her brother." The last statement left me wondering what I might see. Was he an ogre or something?

"G'day, Kate," Kev said when the door opened to his knock. Typical! Kev's favourite sayings is, "You can't change the rules," but he frequently did! "This is Tel," he announced to the little woman in front of me.

"Hello, Kevin. I wasn't expecting you today. Do come in." She was a small, neat woman sporting a tight, plaited bun at the back of her head and a stern wrinkled face. I'd place her in her late sixties, but trying to guess a woman's age is a minefield best avoided by most men.

I furiously cleaned my boots on the welcome mat while wiping my hand on my shorts, before extending it to her, saying, "Pleased to meet you Miss O'Driscoll." She eyed me like a surgeon about to make a serious incision in my neck.

"Something wrong with your feet, son?" She moved aside, saying, "You'd better come in before you wear that mat away." I glanced at Kev for guidance but he'd walked over to where Miss O'Driscoll's brother sat.

I'm glad Kev had warned me about him because it was a disconcerting sight. Frank O'Driscoll had been born with cerebral palsy. His body wasn't under his control and neither were his bodily functions. His tongue was like a monster that kept trying to leave his mouth, making any reasonable conversation almost impossible.

His sister had cared for him all his life. Their parents had died in a flu epidemic and she'd dedicated her life to looking after him. Her care and concern for him were extraordinary.

Kev plonked himself down on a stool next to Frank and wished him a g'day. "Brought a young fella out to meet you, Frank. He's not a bad bloke, considering that he's Greek: he's one of the few of them that actually works!" He gave me a sly grin as Frank ululated with joy.

"He's also got epilepsy." Kev enunciated the word in all the glory of its four syllables. "So if he falls to the floor and starts thrashing around, he's not taking the piss!" In one sentence the man had normalised talking about my condition, established me in the heart of the family and created a bond between me and the O'Driscolls that was to last for the rest of our lives. The man was a bloody genius.

"Ignore him, Tel," Miss O'Driscoll said, "and call me Kate. Pull up a chair and I'll put the kettle on."

"I'll have a beer, thanks," said Kev, giving one of his trademark winks. "All that water'll make me rusty," and he laughed at his own joke. Frank was having a ball!

"It's too early in the day even for scallywags like you, Mr O'Ryan." Kev's eyebrows shot up in mock horror. Behind me I heard the kettle being filled, the scraping sound as Kate placed it on the wood stove, and then the soft hiss that only comes from the cap being taken off the top of a bottle of beer.

"Thanks, Kate," he said when she reappeared and handed him his cold glass, placing the bottle next to him. "I've got your gear in the back of the truck. Where'd you like us to put 'em," he asked, filling his glass from the bottle and taking a long drink out of it. I watched his Adam's apple jerk up and down as he drank and began to think that perhaps beer might be the drink for me, too.

"Would you like some sponge cake, Tel? It only came out of the oven a couple of hours ago. Frank loves his sponge cake, don't you, Frank?" She'd moved to stand next to her brother and was gently twisting her fingers through his greying hair. She spoke her words like a lover, a mother and a sister, such was the deep compassion in her voice. I've never experienced anyone else talk like that. Frank's body stilled under her touch and her words. She fed him the cake spoonful by spoonful, quietly cleaning the crumbs from his chin and his clothes.

"You going to give us a hand, Frank?" Kev asked, causing the writhing to escalate and Frank's eyes to fairly sparkle with delight. We all wished silently that the poor man could – but we all knew that he never would.

"Just leave them out by the shed at the back, Kev," Kate interjected after a pause. "I'm going to put up a new fence around the veggie garden to keep the roos out. They're a damned pest but I'm not going to let anyone shoot them."

"We'll give you a hand," my boss said, polishing off his beer and wiping the foam off his lips. "We've not got much on this arvo, have we, Tel? Between the two of us we should have it knocked off in a couple of hours." I looked at him in stunned disbelief. Only this morning he'd told me that we had a ton of work to do that afternoon and we shouldn't hang around out at the O'Driscolls'!

Digging holes for fence posts sounds easy: take one post-hole shovel, punch it into the ground, pull out a plug of soil and hey, presto, a hole appears! The trouble with that is that God invented rocks, too – and hid most of them in the fence post holes we dug out at the O'Driscolls' place. By the time we'd got the posts in, my shoulders were wrecked from the jarring, my blisters had blisters on them and Kev had finished his sixth bottle of beer. "Makes me a better driver," he said with the customary wink.

Kate had wheeled Frank out and he watched every second of the action with consummate delight. He obviously didn't have much company and he was going to enjoy it. Kate hovered close by him and shooed away any bush fly that dared to approach her beloved brother.

That visit to Kate and Frank O'Driscoll taught me a great deal about life, love and blisters!

We drove back to Yarramah, bumping along the tracks as the sun set in the west in a shout of ruddy glory. Out there in the bush, it got dark pretty quickly, and before long stars began to fill in the deepening, darkening sky.

"We should just make it back to the Royal before closing time," Kev announced above the sound of the motor. "Thirsty work digging holes, eh?" Although I felt his glance on my face, I was a world away trying to piece together the jigsaw of emotions that I'd experienced today. Had Kev planned it all, or did the world just gift me with several very special hours?

That's not football, that's war!

KEV WAS A Trojan worker at whatever he turned his hand to. He'd sweat buckets at the cement works; he'd fry his skin on the roof of a house in the midday sun as he humped up his own cement roof tiles; and he'd fairly frizzle in the paddocks when it came to carting hay for the cockies!

I'd come to think of him as some sort of Superman, so it came as a bit of a surprise when the subject came to talking about footy – after all, he was the team captain. His face would struggle into a grimace, "I'm lazy!" he'd say. "No excuses, Tel, but I don't see the point of it. If you want to win you've gotta go hard. You can't change the rules," he'd incant every Tuesday and Thursday when footy training came around. "I suppose I should go but…" His voice would tail off, his eyebrows rising up towards his receding hairline as if chasing an unsolvable mystery.

"Wouldn't it help if you trained with the team so that you could work out the moves together?" I asked, somewhat naively. "At school we…" I began.

"I don't think there's much to work out," Kev replied, his eyes narrowing to a look which gave the impression of being able to bore through steel. "I'm the captain. All the other blokes have to do is to listen to what I tell 'em! Footy's pretty basic really, you get the ball and you make sure you keep it, then when you get down the other end you kick a goal. Doesn't get much simpler than that," he dared me. "And if they stuff up, then they have to deal with me." He paused for effect. "Seems to be working, seeing as we're top of the table. Must be doing something right," and his wicked grin bloomed in that bullet-shaped noggin of his.

"Maybe I'll come and watch you on Saturday," I offered. Kev flicked me a look that was difficult to decipher.

"Well, you'd better get a wiggle on because these posts aren't going to make themselves," and with that, our conversation was over.

The footy oval was at the end of Lyons Street, the mighty Murray River running along one side of it. It was a beautiful location. Tall trees grew along the river side of the oval, giving the one-eyed, local supporters some decent shade. Nestled in amongst the trees was the local pavilion with seating for the more prosperous, but no less raucous, supporters.

You could always tell there was a game on because on a Saturday morning, most of the locals did their weekly shopping decked out in their blue and white striped footy shirts and matching scarves. At lunchtime, everyone carried Eskies of food and drink down to the oval where the smell of barbecued sausages heralded the start of another gladiatorial encounter. After that, everyone was too busy screaming to notice much else!

Normally there was no way that I could go and watch any home games because I'd be helping Dad out in the shop, but for once he took pity on me. I'd been working non-stop for Kev from dawn until dusk and Dad knew that the break would suit me.

"Don't forget to eat some real food," he said, tossing me a couple of bananas. "Those Aussie sausages are nothing more than burnt skin and fat," which was absolutely ridgy-didge. The local butcher was only two doors up from us and we knew exactly what went into his 'Super Saturday Snaggers'. "And no beer, son. It won't mix with your tablets."

"Yes, Dad." How many times do teenagers say that without ever paying attention to what was being said?

I bumped into Kath just outside the shop as she shuffled her large frame toward the oval. "You going to the match, Tel?" she inquired, as her double chin wobbled in amazement. "Good," she went on, lingering for longer over the middle two vowels than most people would.

I loved Kath. She was fat and cuddly and had the softest heart of anyone in the whole district. She'd cry at anyone's misfortune, but put her near a footy oval where her beloved Yarramah Hawks were playing and beware: the woman became a fanatic and woe betide any opposition players who came within earshot of her! Jekyll and Hyde had nothing on her. Kev told me that she'd been a volunteer during the war in one of the armed services. "She gave great comfort to the men in uniform," he'd say. "Heart of gold. Too big for me, but Kath's a great scout."

The two of us headed to the oval and I found somewhere to sit. Kath went over to where the women's auxiliary were already tending the barbecues and supping on their own supplies of beer. A few of my school mates went past and gave me a regulation 'G'day' before moving on. Legally, they were too young to have a beer but the sound of clinking glass suggested they may have had more than handkerchiefs in their pocket!

"So, you made it, then?" The voice was Kev's. He carried a small kit bag containing his footy things. On top of his kit was a large brown bottle emblazoned with the letters VB. "Liniment," he said. "See you after." He disappeared behind the pavilion to where the changing sheds were. The rest of the team arrived in dribs and drabs – short and tall, fat and skinny, some smoking and some not.

Five minutes before kick off, the Yerringah team bus arrived and pulled up next to the pitch. The front door disgorged a similar style of combatants, all in the process of getting into their playing gear. One stood out. He was a giant of a man, lazily sporting a cigarette in the corner of his mouth. He might have been a smoker, but he had the physique of a Greek god. He was huge!

There was an audible reduction in the chatter around me as all eyes searched the opposition, yet saw just this one man.

"He's a big bastard," seemed to be the consensus amongst the locals.

The whistle blew. It was the signal to the team captains to come and attend the pre-game toss. Hercules, as the Hawks supporters had already nicknamed him, wander over to the centre square. Kev approached from the pavilion looking oddly out of place next to the behemoth. But Kev being Kev, he went right up to the bloke, stuck out his hand and said something. Whatever it was, the big fella went straight for him and the two of them fell to the ground wrestling one another. The little ref from Tuggerama peeped away on his whistle with little success. Eventually, the two men regained their feet and order was restored.

It was Kev who pulled a coin from his pocket and the toss-up was duly consummated. All three peered down at the spot where it landed before Kev pointed to the far end of the paddock, indicating the direction he wanted his team to kick toward. A fleeting thought caused me to smile – maybe it was a double-headed coin they'd just used: I wouldn't put it past the man! The sound of the starting siren brought me into the present moment. The ref bounced the ball and then it was on for young and old.

Considering that these guys were amateurs, they displayed real ball skills and some were unexpectedly speedy. But a lack of fitness and too much smoking eventually marked out several of the players from both sides who struggled to take in enough air after a long run. The younger players, not yet inoculated with bad habits, ran around the place like roos in a truck's headlights. The older, wiser heads were more cunning in their approach, and better skilled in their distribution of the ball.

Kev, for his part, ran as far and as fast as his younger teammates, and always ended up in the right place at the right time. The man was brutal in the tackle zone.

Yet, always standing in the way of the Hawks, was Hercules! The man was unbeatable.

Then, when Hercules had fielded the ball and was about to kick it downfield, there was a blur of blue and Kev caught him with a hip and shoulder. It was a beauty. The two of them hit the ground together and even from the far side of the field you could hear the wind leaving Hercules's lungs.

Kev leaned over him. I thought it may have been be to check if he was still alive, but then he trotted off to his teammates, who crowded around him like a small brood of chicks tweeting around mother hen.

The game turned out to be a fairly even one and it seemed like it was heading for a draw. Then a young roughie from the home team took a mark and headed off towards the Yarramah goal. He out-sprinted most of the defence but as he approached the last man in front of him, you could feel his nerves begin to shred. There was Hercules dancing menacingly from one side to the other right in his path.

Then an amazing thing happened. Hercules froze on one leg, his face scrunched up in agony and he fell down grasping his right leg. "He's done a hammy!" the guy nearest me shouted, as a whoop of delight went up from the locals. The poor kid with the ball almost fell over himself, such was his relief, before he headed into the circle and kicked the winning goal.

The Yerringah team gathered around their fallen totem and supported him as he limped off the field. The Hawks stood at the side of the field and clapped the opposition off. As Hercules went past Kev, he said something to him. I could see that feral expression in Kev's eyes and knew that neither was congratulating the other!

Loitering around a footy field once the action was over was like being the waiter at Banquo's feast. The echoes and ghosts of the action lingered on, but all was empty and quiet. Well, for me it lasted about five minutes before one of my school mates staggered over to offer me a stubby of VB.

"Tel," he slurred, "this'll sort you out. Drink that and at least when you fall over you'll be pissed and not pissing your pants like you normally do." He slapped me across the shoulders, which rattled my teeth and lit a flame under my temper.

I'd heard worse, but it still rankled me. "Smartarse," was my cerebral response. "At least tomorrow when I wake up, I'll know you'll still be stupid!" I watched his face as he struggled to comprehend what I'd just said. "Go home," I said, more in pity than disgust, and walked off.

Kev was on the track at the edge of the pitch as I left. He nodded toward my school buddy as he came to join me. "Sharing his pearls of wisdom with you, is he?" he commented.

"When it comes to nacre, they don't come any duller than Joe," I agreed, quietly chuffed at my play on words.

"For someone who's wet behind the ears, you can be a bit of a smartypants," Kev replied, and we walked along in silence.

"You going back to the Royal?" I asked.

"Yep." Kev can be a man of remarkably few words when he chooses to be.

"Is that big guy OK?" It was a simple question and I expected a simple answer. But with Kev, you have to expect the unexpected!

He sniffed loudly. The suction effect of this action appeared to visibly drag his nose to the right. From my experience at the concrete works, this usually indicated that he was thinking before he spoke – perhaps one of the greatest wisdoms he passed on to me.

"When I was a kid growing up in Coburg, we didn't have much." Kev's eyes narrowed to his gimlet look, yet his arched eyebrows softened his expression as if he were staring at some fond memory in the far distance.

"Dad sold insurance. He used to ride for miles each weekend picking up the subs from families who'd bought policies. Pretty hilly place, Melbourne," he said, sniffing again. I could almost visualise the pictures coming out of his memory. "Footy was pretty big even back then. No telly, just the radio, so you had to make your own entertainment."

We'd reached Lisle Street, where stragglers from the game had congregated on various corners to dissect the game's outcome. Each group gave a happy, "G'day, Kev, great game mate," as we passed by.

"No pocket money back then – well at least there was none where I came from. So a mate of mine called Punter, his real name was Mick, Punter and I'd go down to the local footy ground. I'd pay six pence to get in and Punter'd wait outside the fence. I'd walk around the ground, pick up empty bottles and toss them over the fence to him. Back then you'd get a penny a bottle for returning them."

Kev blinked like an owl before announcing, "I reckon Mick and I made more money than mi' ol' man did," and his features lit up as he laughed out loud. "Punter was big on the horses even when he was a kid. Now he'd bet on two flies crawling up a wall! Bugger if I can remember what I did with mine," he added as he gave a fair impression of a man knocking back a schooner of beer!

We'd arrived at the Royal and he was just about to walk around to the back stairs that led up to his room when I said, "But what about that big bastard who was playing for the opposition?"

Kev's face was classic, and etched itself into my memory.

"That was Punter! He had bet against his team winning and gave me the wink when we tossed up for kick off! I hadn't seen him for ages," he went on as if giving evidence in a trial. "I reckon if he had a quid on the game he'd have won ten in return and Punter never bet less than ten quid at a time – no point really," he expostulated, as if stating the obvious. Looking up the iron fire-escape he announced, "And it wouldn't surprise me if he wasn't already up there in mi' room drinking mi' beer too!" Giving me a theatrical wink, he headed up the steps two at a time.

Gone to sea

MR BONNER WAS a decent sort. I know that a lot of folk in the town gently mocked him behind his back just because he was decent. It's always intrigued me why some people seem to resent what they call 'goodie goodies'. Maybe it's fear? Maybe they're just plain scared that having someone who's trying to be kind, compassionate and caring will show them up to be the mean-spirited people they really are.

Not that Mr Bonner cared. "Don't waste your brain cells worrying about them," he'd say to me and then, more often than not, he'd fold his arms across his broad chest and lean against the nearest wall. I always thought that he did that because he was in the process of settling in to give one of his famous, pithy commentaries on life. I later discovered that it was because of an injury he'd received in a POW camp in Thailand during the war years. Mr Bonner was the wounded healer.

The evening after I'd picked up my first prescription for my epilepsy meds, he had wandered across the street to our shop and taken up his favoured pose against the wall of the cool room, where I was packing away the last few boxes of apples and assorted fruits. "Seems like you got the rough end of the pineapple, Tel," he had said. I heard the click of his Colibri lighter and heard the moist, sucking sound of tobacco being lit in the bulb of his wooden pipe.

"Not much I can do about it, is there?" I replied quietly.

The good man smiled and muttered, "Touché," before slowly releasing a thin stream of smoke which billowed into the cold air in front of him. "Have you ever been sailing, Tel?" The question was harmless, but a thousand threatening thoughts began to buzz inside my head.

"Never thought much about it, Mr Bonner," I replied, somewhat a little defensively.

"Don't worry, lad," he soothed me. "I'm not asking you to sail around the world." He paused for another fix of nicotine. "I have a sailing boat down at the yacht club, down at the end of the Connor's paddock…"

"Yeah," I said. "I've been out that direction a couple of times fishing. Not that it's a great place for fishing, there's too many old logs floating around the edge around there."

The Murray River had been dammed earlier in the century to create a huge artificial lake. The ghostly forest of dead trees standing shoulder deep in water stood as a tribute to the amazing endurance of the massive river red gum trees. But from time to time, a branch would fall or a whole tree topple, threatening danger to passing speed boats or to the tackle of unsuspecting fishermen.

"Maybe you'd like to come out with me sometime." He dislodged himself from his support and turned to leave without waiting for an answer.

"Thanks, Mr Bonner," I shouted at his retreating figure. "I'd like that."

The aging pharmacist turned back to me giving me an inquisitive look. "I'll hold you to that, Tel," he said, and walked off leaving a trail of smoke corkscrewing behind him.

It had been a few weeks since the footy game against Yerringah, and many of the locals were still arguing the toss as to how come the Hawks had actually won, when Mr Bonner called to me from across the street.

"I hear the weather forecast says that the wind will be coming from the east this arvo, Tel. Should be a great time for a spot of sailing. Interested?"

Dad, who'd been up since 3 am on one of his twice-weekly Melbourne runs to re-stock the shop, looked across at me. I could see how tired he was. I was on the verge of shouting back, "Thanks, but..." when Dad shouted back to him, "What time, Mr Bonner?"

"How about I meet Tel at the yacht club around two o'clock?" A quick thumbs up from Dad sealed the deal.

"Dad," I began, but he stopped me with the palm of his hand.

"You deserve it son. After all, it's not often you get asked out on a yacht," he smiled.

Dad and I hug each other – it's a Greek thing – so I went over to him and we probably gave each other the best hug recorded that year in north east Victoria.

I soon found out that Yarramah yacht club was not Monte Carlo! It was a tin shed at the side of the lake with a small jetty and a few aging boats tied up to it. Mr Bonner was already on his little boat, struggling to step the mast.

"Grab hold of it, Tel, and I'll fix the stays," he ordered like the real captain of a real yacht. The highly unstable wooden craft I stepped onto was about twelve foot long and about three times as many years old. But you could see that to Mr Bonner, not even a gilded cabin below decks could have made it any finer. He fixed the stays in place with much grunting and readjustment of his blue, peaked cap. Stepping back, he admired the mast and watched the pennant flag flap at its summit.

The wind was definitely picking up because straight away the lead wires for the mainsail began to slap the metal mast with a demented yet rhythmic beat.

"Looks like a good day for a sail, eh?" Mr Bonner said, looking up from attaching the foresail and fixing the ropes of the mainsheet into the cleats. Not being a sailor myself, I had to agree with him, but the speed with which the gathering low clouds were scudding across the sky raised a sense of uncertainty in my mind. Even though we lived next door to a lake, I wasn't what you'd call a strong swimmer and at this time of year the water was bloody cold!

With the mainsail now furiously flapping in the strengthening wind, Mr Bonner's face took on the expression of Toad in *Toad of Toad Hall* when he first saw a motor car. There was a transition from benevolent pharmacist to manic devotee to the art of insane sailing.

"Anchors away!" he shouted from the tiller, while pulling on a rope used to sheet in the mainsail. Immediately, the boom swung around with great force, nearly decapitating me in the process.

"Stay sharp, Tel," my captain shouted, "We're off!" The old wooden vessel responded like a puppy let loose in the park. "The first time sailing is always the most memorable," Captain Bonner yelled as I took refuge on the side of the boat furthest from the water. "That's the way lad, balance the boat for me while I get the foresail fixed." It was a relief to know that my instinct for the preservation of life – namely my own – was also considered good seamanship!

"Aye aye, Captain!" I shouted back, briefly feeling that this sailing lark was going to be easier than I thought.

We had barely gone fifty yards before there was a loud 'thwang' and the boom swung out wide, allowing the mainsail to fill with a huge lungful of now near-cyclonic wind. I looked at Mr Bonner with real dread in my heart. "What was that?" I shouted.

"Oh dear," he said looking a tad crestfallen. "The boom vang just broke." Maybe it was the mixture of mild disappointment and complete mystification that led him to add, "It's the rope used to tie the boom in position." Sensing I was no wiser, he added, "It means I can't control the mainsail. All we can do is run before the wind or…" By now the water was spilling over the rails of the boat as she sped along like an out-of-condition dog chasing a very fast rabbit.

Mr Bonner began to scrabble about below his seat and then tossed something at me. It looked like an old life jacket from World War I. The smile on my face at his sense of humour faded when I looked back at him.

"You'd better put it on Tel, just in case."

"Just in case of…?" Enlightenment hit me in the face like the cold water that was now lapping around my feet. As my head appeared through the orifice of the jacket I was putting on, I found myself staring at the stark graveyard of drowned trees which once lived in this place before man killed them. And to my panicked mind, they looked set on getting their revenge!

"Hold on, Tel," he yelled, "looks like we're heading towards the trees."

By now, the lake had been whipped into a frenzy and white caps madly rode next to us, urging our small boat on towards certain destruction.

Without any warning the small boat keeled over and we landed in the water. The cold water may have frozen my body, but my mind remained icily clear. I tried to come up to the surface but something was holding me down. I managed to push my face a few inches above the waves before I realised that I was under the mainsail. Luckily, my WWI lifejacket was as useless as an ashtray on a motorbike, so I was able to duck dive under the water again and swim away to open water.

Once clear of the sail I found myself too close to the trees for comfort. Mr Bonner was climbing onto the upturned wreck and urging me to swim over to him as we were driven closer and closer toward the trees. I took a swift look to see how far away the shore was, but it seemed miles away. Panic began to rise in my chest and then I think I fainted and slipped below the surface.

It felt like only a millisecond, and then I was being dragged over the side of the boat. The sun had come out, which warmed my back. I assumed that the storm had passed, which was a good thing, and then my mind was slammed with an avalanche of thoughts.

If my back feels warm, where is my shirt? In fact, where is that useless life jacket?

If I'd been under water for the length of time it had taken for a normal storm to pass, how come I felt so fresh?

Was that the hoot of an owl I just heard?

And finally, why was the bottom of this boat so different to the bottom of Mr Bonner's boat? This one had seats down the length of it from which dangled several pairs of legs.

I popped my head above the gunwale and gazed across a glistening, cerulean sea. The horizon merged into the palest of blue skies where the occasional gull circled silently overhead. I sat back on my heels, scanning up and down the boat. Bare-chested young men with olive tanned skin and tousled, salt encrusted hair sat at each bench staring at me. A shadow loomed over me and a familiar voice asked, "I don't think we were formally introduced, Tel."

I looked up into the sunlight and saw the black outline of a man. From the shimmering light that glistened off his arms, I assumed that this was the person who'd pulled me on board. He shifted slightly, allowing his face to come into view. Before I was able to say a word, he reached out to me and introduced himself. "It's Mentor. We met briefly at the house of Laertes."

My mind reacted like a mob of sheep trying to leave a sheep pen all at once. The result: confusion and inertia. It felt like I was attempting to lever out the deeply embedded thought that Kev doesn't like boats and that he was about to say 'G'day' … but my tongue remained still in my open mouth.

Mentor pulled me up and held me by the shoulders. "When the gods come amongst us, you must be prepared for the unexpected. It seems that that great comforter of Odysseus has come to your aid, Telemecus. Be happy that wise Athene has befriended you. With her as your benefactor, what may seem impossible can often come to pass."

I heard his whispered words, yet it seemed that Mentor's lips remained still in a sealed smile. In that moment I realised that the time for asking questions had passed.

One of the sailors passed me a leather flask of fresh water. I nodded back in appreciation and took a deep lug of the refreshingly cold liquid. "Is Telemecus here?" I asked, hoping beyond hope that he was. A familiar face would go a long way to settling my confusion and, truth be told, I'd missed having him around, despite his propensity for impulsive behaviour. I could just imagine Dad saying, "Kids these days...!"

"Greetings, Alexander," his familiar voice hailed me from the stern of the boat, where he held firm to the tiller. "You certainly know how to make a grand entrance! How did you know we had been seeking my father, noble Odysseus himself?"

I was on the point of saying that I'd read the book, but instead I shrugged. "Intuition I guess."

Mentor squeezed my shoulder gently and returned to his place at the bow of the boat. I moved back to Telemecus and took my place on the empty bench next to him. "He's the strong silent type, isn't he?" I said to my friend, nodding in the direction of Mentor.

Telemecus gazed quietly at the old man. "I've known him all my life and never has he failed me. Certainly that man has been touched by the gods."

Seeing as I'd just been pulled from the waters by a band of random Greek guys from 3,000 years ago, I thought it perhaps not the right time to take the piss about believing in gods and fairies. He just might not take it in the right way!

"So, where are we off to?" I asked as brightly as I could, having determined that there was no point in asking hypothetical questions when the hard facts were all around me!

"It's a long story. The gods be praised that at least I have Mentor to advise me." Telemachus gazed up at the sail as if seeing the very wind itself. "Nothing has changed since I saw you last. The suitors continue to lay waste to our home, eating our food, drinking our wine, wooing my beloved mother Penelope and telling her that Odysseus is dead. Then one night the goddess Athene came to me in a dream…"

"Yeah. I've had some of those dreams myself."

Ignoring my interruption, he went on. "And she urged me to visit my father's old friends, Nestor and Menelaus, who fought alongside him in the long war against Troy. So I took a boat with the aid of old Mentor there, and we set out to seek news of him."

Something deep in my own soul stirred as he spoke. I have the dearest and best parents in the world, but the sad fact is that they aren't my real parents. Never once had it occurred to me to find out who they really were. And yet here was my new mate Telemachus, who hadn't stopped wondering about his old man for the past twenty years, and was setting out across some pretty treacherous waters to find news of him. I was gobsmacked!

"Are you alright, Alexander?" my friend asked. "Forgive me for ignoring your ordeal. How long were you in the water before we found you? And what were you doing there?" His voice tapered off as the strangeness of my appearance began to arouse that worm of doubt.

Being an Aussie, I had learned to think on the run. "Actually, I heard an owl hooting and then, *poof*, I was swimming around Ithaca." I smiled like a buffoon back at him.

For some reason, he believed me. "Athene," was all he said.

Before he could have another irritating thought, I asked, "So, did you get any news?"

"Strange tidings we got certainly, although no-one has seen Odysseus in all that time. We heard that he left Troy after the citadel fell, and took ship back to Ithaca. But the gods were angry and blew him way off course. After many adventures with the Scylla, the Charybdis, Cyclops and the bewitching sirens he was stranded on the island of Ogygia with the goddess Calypso, who has kept him a prisoner there. Yet by all accounts, despite her captivating beauty, my father still yearns for home and his wife Penelope. Wise Menelaus tells me that the gods have relented and that great friend of Odysseus, Athene, has helped him speed his way back to Ithaca even as we speak. I also hear that the suitors plan to ambush us as we return, and murder us in our boat so that they can seize my home and lands."

Telemachus smiled and put his arm around my shoulder. "If it weren't for the gods, Alexander, I would be at the bottom of the sea and you'd still be swimming around in circles!"

I looked him in the eye. Then the two of us burst out laughing until our bellies ached. The rest of the crew smiled at our stupidity while Mentor sat shrouded beneath his hood, his shoulders gently shaking, which only made us laugh even more.

A day later, one of the crew sighted land. The sails were loosened and the men rowed us to the shore with Telemachus guiding us in. As we approached the beach, the anchor stone was thrown overboard and we waded up onto the sand. Once safely ashore, we followed the Greek tradition of celebrating a safe return home by mixing wine and preparing food. Mum would have been in her element here!

Speaking to the whole crew, Telemachus announced, "After you've eaten and drunk you must take the boat around to the town without me. This is where I will leave you as I need to visit one of our herdsmen to hear how things stand with the suitors. Tomorrow I will come to the city and give you all a good meal and some fine wine to thank you for your help."

It's funny, but even though I knew what was going to happen – fighting, death and mayhem – I couldn't help myself and whispered to Telemachus, "Sorry, mate, but I'm tagging along with you. This is going to be fun!" Mentor too slipped away from the crew and walked on ahead of us.

Soon we could hear the sound of pigs.

"We must be nearing the home of Eumaeus," Telemachus said happily. "He has been as a father to me since my own left these many years since. I will go there to hear what news he has. You and Mentor must go to my grandfather Laertes and tell of our news. He will have grieved at my going, but will rejoice at my safe return. Meet me in the town tomorrow when we will sacrifice to the gods, mix wine and celebrate our journey."

Telemachus embraced us both before turning off the path and heading towards a small shack with a smaller lean-to on one side. Smoke was coming from a fire, which meant that there would be someone to greet him. The last I saw of him was being happily met by Eumaeus' dogs, which made no sound upon his arrival.

"They must be old friends, eh, Mentor?" I said to my companion.

"Faithful friends come in many guises," he said in his low, rumbling voice. It made me smile to always associate his face with Kev's and expect him to talk to me like, well, er … Kev.

We walked on and soon came to lands which were well-husbanded, with well-kept orchards and well-dressed vines. "Laertes has ever loved the land and cared for it these many decades. He taught your friend's father many things about the land and they planted many trees together. I wonder, should Odysseus ever return from his long journey, would he recognise those saplings which he planted and which are now full grown trees?"

As we walked, we came across the field to where the old cottage stood. Standing next to it was old Laertes looking like a beggar. He wore old clothes and had leather thongs bound around both arms and legs. On his head he wore what appeared to be a battered leather fez, similar to one I'd once seen in a sepia picture of an Afghan camel driver from the nineteenth century. Laertes was slowly cutting lengths of brambles from a straggling bramble bush and piling them to one side. "Has he gone soft in the head?" I asked in a weak attempt at humour.

Mentor chuckled softly to himself. "I doubt it," he replied. "Strange as it may seem, that man is wiser than most men on Ithaca yet he seems greatly faded since last I saw him. Much has he grieved at the departure of Telemachus. May he be greatly restored by his return. Come, let us go to him and relieve him of his pains."

"But what's with harvesting brambles?" I asked sotto voce. "Is it some local bush that ferments into an exotic beverage?"

This time it was Mentor's time to laugh. "You have much to learn and even more to unlearn, young Telemachus. No, Laertes is harvesting the brambles to use around his pig pens. It keeps the pigs in and the wild beasts out. Everything that appears evil can often be turned to good use … if you have the will and the patience."

"And leather undies, too," I smiled back at him. From the blank expression on his face, I understood that leather undies were not part of the Ancient Greek lexicon. "Don't worry," I added as we approached old Laertes.

"What news, Laertes?" Mentor announced in the voice most of us use for older folk. The aged man turned his face towards us. Tears were streaming down his furrowed cheeks. His rheumy old eyes were bloodshot with crying. He sniffed and wiped his nose on his leather sleeves, streaking a smudge of dirt across his face, adding more pathos to his expression. Mentor bent down and helped him to his feet. "Dear Laertes, we come with good news. Telemachus is home. As we speak he is with Eumaeus learning of how things stand with Penelope and the suitors". The delight and relief that surfaced on his features was like the sunrise of a rosy fingered dawn.

"So it's true," he said so softly. "Last night in my dreams that great friend of my son, the ever faithful Athene, appeared. She told me to clear away the accumulated canker of despair, for with the dawn, hope would arise like freshly sprouting wheat after spring rains had broken a long drought."

He reminded me of old Frank Lambert when he had come home from hospital after he'd been kicked by a cow. He'd broken his leg and was pretty crook. "Bloody lucky it wasn't mi' head," he had said to Dad. Good bloke, Frank.

"Come in, come in," Laertes said, scurrying towards his old home. "We must mix wine and give thanks to Zeus and his daughter Athene for such great news, and you must tell me as much as you know."

"Hold hard, dear friend." Mentor stopped him with a firm grip of his shoulder. "There is more to tell. Telemachus brought news that Odysseus is on his way home. He may even have arrived before us and be with his long besieged wife Penelope as we speak."

The look on the old man's face would make a stone weep with joy. In an instant his eyes had gone from sparkling excitement to the size of Mum's favourite blue-rimmed dinner plates and brimming with tears. He collapsed into the arms of wise Mentor, where the poor man sobbed his sweet heart out.

Then the cold stone of sadness appeared in my heart. Is this how a father really feels about his son? I knew Dad loved me with every fibre of his being, but he wasn't my real dad. Was my real dad out there somewhere feeling the same way as Laertes was feeling just now? In that moment I made a promise to myself that by hook or by crook, I would find out who my real parents were, but without letting on to Dad and Mum, because I knew if they found out, it might break their hearts.

When Laertes had recovered himself, we mixed the wine, toasted the gods and had a small feast in his ramshackle old cabin. It was a shame Mum wasn't there as she'd have rustled up something that would make the old man's stomach creak with comfort. AND she'd have had this place ship-shape in no time at all. I must have looked as if I was spaced out while I was thinking about Mum, because when I paid attention again, the two older men were looking at me in a benign sort of way.

"Telemachus here has had a difficult journey and I think needs a rest." Old Laertes went into a corner where some of his brambles were gathered. I looked in alarm at Mentor, who merely smiled back. Then Laertes brought in sheepskins, with which he covered the brambles, thus producing what was probably the original inner sprung mattress. The man's a genius!

Graciously thanking him, I took one last sip of the freshly mixed wine and lay down on the freshly made bed. The heady scent which arose from the crushed brambles mixed with the warming effect of the wine sent me into the deepest sleep in what must have been world record time.

A second
awakening

DREAMS ARE STRANGE things. They don't ever seem to start, you sort of find yourself in the middle of the 'production' and never ever think about what went before, or even what is going to happen next – you're just suddenly in the middle of it.

In this dream, I was down at Gordon's Bends on the Murray. Tall river red gums soared high overhead with scattered collections of leaves rattling in the evening breeze. I heard an owl call, which is not that common on the Murray. Cockies, crows and ducks were the usual birds around those parts, but in a dream anything goes! Then there was a beautiful woman standing there. I don't think she said anything but I knew something, something that changed my life forever. Athene smiled at me, because she knew that I knew. Suddenly, I was so deliriously happy that I choked.

In fact, I choked a good few times. "You certainly know how to frighten the life out of your parents, young man!" I knew that voice!

Opening my eyes, I saw a bright round light shining down on me. I flicked my eyes to the right, and bingo, there she was: my beautiful Irish nurse. "We never did get introduced," I said, assuming my standard suave grin.

I swiftly ascertained that I was back in the small casualty area of Yarramah District Hospital. The theatre light looked down at me like a myopic cyclops. "Well, you've got a very odd way of getting to know people," she said, looking down at her nurse's watch strategically placed on her starched uniform. Holding my wrist with her cold fingers, she flashed a look at me. The old Tel began to stir.

"You'd better wipe that smile off your face before your mother arrives. I'm not sure who's in more trouble, you or Mr Bonner." She picked up a chart and wrote something. "What day is it today?"

"Tuesday."

"What month is it?"

"September."

"Who's the Prime Minister?"

"Who cares?" That stern look returned to her pretty face.

"I don't know his name and come to think of it, I don't know yours, either." Another of those looks.

"Mr Alysandratos, you're an epileptic, you've just been pulled out of a lake in a raging storm, you've got a probable head injury and all you can think of is chatting up your nurse-in-charge, whose name happens to be Sue McDermott," she announced in a semi-serious tone.

"Three out of four isn't bad," I volunteered. That confused her.

"I beg your pardon," she replied.

"I said three out of four isn't bad. Yes, I was pulled out of a lake in a raging storm – it was bloody scary out there." My recent liaison with a voracious expanse of cold water flooded back, if you can excuse the pun. "By the way, how is Mr Bonner? Is he OK? And yes, I think I did hit my head on something and yes, your name is Sue McDermott because I can see it on your name badge." Pausing for dramatic effect and grinning like the idiot, I gave my final pronouncement: "But no, I don't have epilepsy."

It looked like Sue was worried the head injury might have been worse than originally thought, because she took a step back. Taking on a very professional air, she picked up my chart, saying, "Dr Buckley will be in after surgery and he'll talk to you then. In the meantime, you'd better get some rest." She patted me gently on my hand, which was quite sweet really.

A part of me felt for her because she didn't know what I knew. Then slowly the thoughts came buzzing into my head like a mob of early springtime blowflies. Who'd believe me? How could I be so certain? It was a dream … wasn't it? Doubt oozed under the slim veneer of my hope.

I would have had plenty of time to slowly stew in my own thoughts as Doc Buckley didn't get away from surgery until after six, but Mum arrived and she was not in a happy place.

"My poor son, they try to kill you again. What is it with these bloody Australians?" That certainly focused my attention fairly smartly. Mum never, ever swore so she must have been really upset. "If Bonner not drowned yet, then maybe I go and finish the job!"

"Mum," I interjected, "it wasn't his fault. One of the ropes broke and the boat just took off on its own accord. There was nothing Mr Bonner could do." Recognising that I was not making any headway, I added, "And it was Mr Bonner who saved me. If it hadn't been for him, I'd be…" and I drew my fingers across my throat whilst dramatically rolling my eyes up through the top of my head.

"Maybe," she relented a bit, "but why the crazy man go out when the lake is…" Her vocabulary failed her.

"That's Australia for you, Mum. Perfect one minute and wanting to kill you the next. Remember the snake Dad found in the crate of bananas?" This was always a winner and sent the dear woman into paroxysms of shudders. "And it's amazing how those red-back spiders have enough venom in them to kill a horse and yet all they do is catch flies." I shook my head in mock wonder.

By now Mum was distracted enough to have overcome her abject fear that she might have lost her beloved son. She leaned forward and buried my face in her ample and very loving bosom.

"If anything happened to my Telemachus…" Her voice trailed off as tears welled in her eyes.

"Don't worry about me, Mum. I'm like one of those Greek heroes from history. I've got a god on my side." I immediately sensed that I may have stepped over an invisible line. Mum didn't say anything. She didn't need to. She just looked at me with one of those looks.

She muttered some Greek imprecation under her breath while crossing herself in the Orthodox way before asking, "You sure you're OK?"

"I'm fine, Mum," I said, grabbing her free hand. "It's a joke." I knocked on my skull, saying, "Pure red gum," and smiled sweetly back at her. That worried look remained locked on her face. "Honest, Mum, I feel absolutely fine," I pleaded. Maybe I was a little too earnest or perhaps it was her intuition, but I am certain that deep inside, a worry worm had been disturbed.

"My son, you need to rest. I go and talk with your father. Maybe tomorrow you come home. See what Dr Buckley say." She then did something she'd never done before: she made the sign of the cross on my forehead and then kissed me there as if to make sure it sank in properly.

"Thanks, Ma," I said. "I love you."

"I love you too, son." And then she was gone.

Doubt is the cataract that distorts the clear sight of hope. Once established it can be a bugger to get rid of. The worst thing is to suppress the idea of doubt and pretend that it never happened. All that does is allow it to continue its cancerous course and silently infect other areas of your thinking. Naturally, I decided to stay silent!

By the time the good doctor finally arrived, I'd come to the conclusion that the least I said about epilepsy, the better. Once I'd got home, I'd work out some plan and then everything would be sorted out.

Doc Buckley had other ideas. He looked tired and drawn and I suppose he was waiting to get home and have his tea. Maybe it was that which made him seem a tad grumpy. "What's all this rubbish about you not having epilepsy, Tel? Didn't I explain to you, at great length may I say, that it's something you've got for life and the sooner you get used to it the better for all concerned? And for goodness sake, don't go repeating this drivel to your parents, they've got enough on their plate as it is."

Pithy, I thought.

"Sorry, Doc," was my humble response. "I was just having a bit of fun with Sue here."

That must have confused him a bit but then the penny dropped. Actually, it must have been an iron bar! "This is Sister McDermott to you, Tel, and you treat her with the greatest of professional courtesy, you hear? Now take your medicine and go to sleep." Turning to Sister McDermott, he grumped, "I'll review him in the morning and if everything's OK then he can go home. Ring me if you have any problems with him." The last words were spoken as he glared down at me.

There was something very vulnerable about being flat on my back in a hospital bed tightly swaddled by a stiff white sheet and an antiseptic smelling hospital blanket!

"Geez," I said when Sue came back, "he's a bit antsy, isn't he? I don't fancy Mrs B will be too happy if he goes off at her like he did to me just now." The whole town knew that Mrs Buckley was a formidable figure and kept the good doc on a tight reign. Maybe that's why he let go at some of his patients from time to time – just to feel like he had a bit of power after all.

"Dr Buckley has had a long day, and it's not an easy job dealing with sickness and suffering every day, young man. When you've got your health, you've found your wealth, as my Mammy often says." A flicker of hurt made her left eye close just a little bit as she realised that she had just said that I wasn't as rich as I thought I was. Passing me a small glass pill jar with my regular medications, she reached across to my bedside locker and poured me a glass of water. "Come on now, Tel, time for your tablets."

"Thanks, Sister," I said, over-emphasising the word and flashing her a grin at the same time.

"You're incorrigible, Tel," Sue said, taking back the jar and the glass from me. "I'll check on you later." She had reached the ward door when she added, "Oh, I forgot. Your mum left you a book. It's in your locker." With that, she was gone.

I lay there breathing in Sue's lingering scent, which had ebbed out of her hair as she'd given me the glass of water. I immediately thought of Athene, and hope returned to polish my lens on life.

Beauty, love, and healing. Now there's something to let your troubled mind rest its thoughts on.

I loosened the sheets and twisted to retrieve the book Mum had left for me. "Ha," I said out loud. Flopping back on the bed, I opened the much-thumbed, dog-eared friend of my youth. Inside the front cover was Dad's spidery writing: "To Telemachus, with all our love and hope, Dad and Mum xx". It'd been my tenth birthday gift from them. That book had filled my dreams and linked the giants of the past with the giants that I knew lived in my own mind.

"Thanks, Ma," I said, again out loud, thumbing to the later chapters of Homer's classic book.

"Are you talking to yourself, Tel? They say that's the first sign of madness." I knew the voice straight away. The owner of that redoubtable voice was Mr Kelly, who ran the hardware store. I hadn't realised there was anyone else in the room. It was a four-bed ward and the curtain next to me was drawn across, separating me from the disembodied voice. The two beds opposite were empty.

"Is that you, Mr Kelly?" I asked lightly. "What are you doing here?"

"Hole in one, Tel. Why am I here? It's a somewhat sensitive subject, actually, so keep it under your hat please. Haemorrhoids!"

That wasn't a word I was conversant with so I let silence answer for me.

"I'm having surgery on my backside tomorrow. Doc suggested I come in tonight so that I don't eat anything that might upset his anaesthetic gases." Mr Kelly was a good friend of Kev's, which spoke volumes for his recreational pastimes at the Royal, which were 99% of the time of the liquid variety.

"Enough said, Mr Kelly. I've already forgotten what you said."

"I thought Doc was a bit tough on you mate. Did you pinch his golf clubs or something?"

"Nah. It's just a misunderstanding." Changing the subject I asked if he'd seen Kev recently.

"Not really. He's been carting wheat out at a place over near K'rang," he answered matter-of-factly. "I think he's been staying with a cobber of his over that way. They say the bloke brews the best beer in north east Victoria, so I suppose it'll be a long job, knowing Kev!" He laughed in a raucous, raspy voice loud enough to stir Sister Sue to pop her head in the door.

"Quieten down you two. You'll be upsetting the babies in the nursery with the racket you're making," she admonished with her barely twenty-year-old authority. "I'll be in with your sleeping tablets shortly, Mr Kelly." She shot me a friendly look and whispered, "Are you OK in here with him, Tel?" I winked back at her and gave her the thumbs up. "Lights out in thirty minutes, gentlemen." And with that she was gone.

Sleeping with a strange man on the other side of the curtain was something new to me. The dear man slept like a log, snored like a bull and passed the most wicked wind I had ever smelled.

But the night nurse made the black hours pass easily. She invited me into the nurses' station and made me a delicious hot chocolate. She told me her name, but it didn't stick – it's a weakness of mine. I'd remember a face for years, but names seemed to slip through my memory like vague shadows. That nurse sat and listened to my stories with a gentle, believing expression on her lined face. I'd say she was in her late fifties. All I remember is that she was married to a cocky out in bush somewhere. He had bad lungs and she needed to work so that they didn't lose the farm. A common enough story in the country.

She exuded an aura of trust and at some point during the deep hours of the night I told her of my dreams. She sipped her tea quietly and said nothing.

In the morning before Sue came back on duty, the night nurse came around to check on us all and provide those who needed them with bed pans and toiletries. She came to me and tidied my bed, tucking my sheets firmly under the mattress.

"There are some dreams you must follow, Tel. They're the ones that you decide upon when you're awake. There are other dreams that are telling you something about yourself: those you must listen to. Then there are those rare dreams that come from somewhere so very special that they can affect your whole life." She stood there for a few seconds as if looking into my mind with her gentle, grey eyes. "Sue'll be in soon. She'll get you ready for discharge," and she left.

"Mark my words, Tel," Mr Kelly's voice came from behind the curtain, "she's a bloody good sort. You ask Kev about her when you see him. An' tell him I haven't forgotten about his pick for the 3.30 at Albury last week. Tell him I owe him one."

"Sure will, Mr Kelly," I replied. I think his pre-med must have kicked in then because the rhythmic sound of his loud snoring soon filled the ward.

True to form, Sue arrived, and then about an hour later, Doc arrived, scurrying busily into the room and causing the curtains to flap in his wake.

"How are you feeling today, Tel?" he inquired perfunctorily while picking up the chart from the end of my bed. He studied it with a furrowed brow and then came and took my pulse. "Hmm. You look pretty fit to me. Want to go home?"

"Sure do, Doctor," I smiled back at him.

"Right. Make sure he has enough medication, Sister, and I'll see him in a month at the surgery. You will remember to come, won't you?" he challenged me.

"Yes, Doc."

He made a sort of harrumph sound, scratched an invisible spot on his cheek and went off to see his next patient.

By the time Sue had returned about a quarter of an hour later, I was sitting fully dressed on the side of my bed, my hospital pyjamas neatly folded on the pillow. Her eyes opened wide in mock admiration. "I never took you to be house proud, Tel. I'm impressed. For an only child, and a Greek one as well, that's pretty impressive."

"I'm an Aussie, Sue, and Greek Aussies are a very impressive species." I stared into her lovely eyes and I really think that she blushed.

"Pick your medications up at the desk and don't forget to see the doctor in a month's time."

"Maybe we'll catch up in town sometime," I dared to suggest.

"And maybe not," was her quick retort.

In ten minutes, I was walking out the front door of the hospital onto Lyons Street, sucking in great lungfuls of fresh air. Leaving hospital after being an in-patient is one of the better experiences in life. An even better one is never having to go in as a patient in the first place!

As I walked down the street to the shop, I began to wonder how I could solve the two great mysteries of my life: who were my real parents, and did I really have epilepsy? Both were fraught with dire consequences, such as breaking Mum and Dad's hearts, and losing the respect of just about everyone in town.

The initial delight at going home was severely dampened as the loneliness bird laid another stone egg in my heart.

One mystery solved

SUMMER WAS OVER and school was back in full swing. It was my final year and I was expected to do well even though the medications played havoc with my concentration. Life swiftly developed its own tempo: up early to help Dad get the shop ready, eat the big breakfast that Mum always thought I needed – "A growing boy needs his food," she'd intone each day before packing my lunch up and then packing me off for school.

"Thanks, Mum," would be the ritual response. As it turned out, those lunches were tradable commodities. The other kids loved the sweet baklava, which was great because I have a savoury tooth, and besides which, it kept me in pocket money during term time. I suppose it's what comes from being the son of a Greek shopkeeper! It also stopped me from turning into a human blob.

When I could, I'd make a detour on the way home past Kev's concrete works. His little radio was like the open/closed sign on most of the other shops. When it was on, I'd go inside and do some sweeping up or just stack some trestles and posts. I called it my charity work. After all, I didn't want him to miss his afternoon tea, did I?

On this particular day, he said, "You're a bloody good bloke, Tel," while taking a large pull from a bottle of water that he had on the floor nearby. "So what's your problem?" Kev was never one to hold back on any subject.

"Not much really, Kev," I replied, putting the yard brush back where it was kept neatly with all his other tools – Kev's a stickler for tidiness. He gave me one of his 'If that's all you're going to say, you may as well bugger off now and stop wasting my time' looks. I struggled to think of a way to explain my conundrum.

"I'm adopted," was all I managed to blurt out. The Beatles were singing on Kev's radio, *"I've told you before, you can't do that!"* Suddenly I felt sick.

"So bloody what?" Kev asked with what sounded to be genuine surprise. Over time I'd become more comfortable with Kev's way of communicating. When he sounded pissed off with you, he was actually imparting some serious advice. Just now he sounded seriously pissed off!

"Tel," he began, "you're bloody lucky to have two parents. Believe me, there's a ton of kids growing up without any parents at all. Then there're the ones whose old men were killed in the last great war, and now the bastards in Parliament are packing the next lot off to Vietnam to come back either dead or mushed up in their minds. How would you like your old man to be maimed or off his rocker? And how would your mum cope, especially if she had to deal with a boofhead like you as well!"

"I know," I whined back at him. But I didn't.

As if to bang the point home with a large mallet he added, "Remember Jacko Thompson? His kids go to your school. He was in Vietnam. Three weeks after he got back he blew his brains out down the bends at Trawala." Kev filled a shovel with some cement and dumped it into a new mould. The scraping sound it made accentuated my sense of sickness. "They're the ones doing it tough, Tel."

"You're right, Kev," I conceded. "Dad and Mum have been the best parents a bloke could ever have. It's just..."

"What?" The word sounded like a backside being smacked with a large bat!

"Well, perhaps my real parents might have changed their mind and..." my voice trailed off.

Kev eyed me like a chicken eyes a fat worm that is too slow to squeeze back down its hole. "So what's your plan, genius?"

The question left me exposed. I'd been thinking about who my real parents might be, but when it came down to the nitty gritty, I had no idea about how to go about finding them. I daren't ask my parents because it would break their hearts. I really had only one option.

"I thought I'd ask you to help me, Kev," I muttered weakly.

Kev has a deep nature yet most people think he's just an overgrown larrikin who drinks too much and is over fond of female company. I suppose that in two out of three cases they're right, but Kev's more than that: much, much more.

"So, smartypants, you seem to have worked out that you need a mum and a dad in order to have children. An' living in God's own country, which seems to like keeping a record on just about everything except my wages, it seems to me that somewhere there must be records of that disastrous day when you popped your head into the world." He looked pretty fierce, but I knew he was joking. Not about how much he earned, though. Most of that was cash or 'in kind' payments, which usually came in a liquid form.

My spirits began to lift. "What are you trying to say, Kev?"

"In Melbourne there's a thing called a Registry of Births, Marriages and Deaths. Your name'd have to be in there somewhere, that's if they have a section for dopey Greek kids as well." And in an instant that crazy Kev O'Ryan grin appeared. Geez, I loved the man.

"How do I get there, Kev? Where is it? Do you know where it is?" The questions tumbled out of my mouth. But the door to Kev's heart shut just as quickly as it opened. He bent over his form and began trowelling the wet cement.

"If you think I'm going to drop everything and head off on a wild goose chase just because some wet behind the ears kid gets a mad idea in his head..." Fixing me with one of those looks he threatened, "You'd better smarten up young fella, and be quick about it."

The granular sound of the trowel as it slid over the sides of the metal mould were like white noise to my thinking. "Now bugger off home and help your dad in the shop before it gets dark," Kev said without looking up. And that was the end of the conversation.

"See ya, Kev," I said. "Thanks, mate. Talk to you later." Automatic words to fill the void that lay between us.

Mum was out the back gathering some veggies to cook for our evening meal. Dad was serving the last straggling customers before the streets emptied, leaving the dogs to clean up any leftovers. When I'd finished my chores there was still about half an hour before tea. I asked if I could go down to the foreshore for a walk to clear my head before I began my homework.

"Don't keep your mother waiting, Tel," Dad offered with a knowing look.

"Sure thing, Dad," and with that I wandered down the street.

The western sky clung to the palest of blues, while in the east a spreading gloom inexorably dissolved all before it.

"It's like my bloody life," I said out loud, not thinking that anyone else might be nearby.

"You sound like you've had a bad day, Tel," a voice said. This voice was a familiar voice that instantly sent a thrill through me, expunging all dark thoughts from my mind.

"What's a nice girl like you doing in a place like this?" I said to Sue, whose bright smile restored my faith in my Greek genes.

"I might say the same about you, young man," she retorted with appropriate Celtic charm. "You didn't sound too bright just a second ago, though," and there was genuine concern in her voice. She came over from the bench where she'd been sitting watching the sun sink lower in the west and slipped her arm through mine. It was a thing I was to learn about Irish girls: they have an easy familiarity that is devoid of sexual intent – well, mostly, that is!

"Let's walk a little," she suggested, and that's just what we did.

Sue had a simplicity that belied a deep intelligence and it was so easy just to walk with her. She was like a big sister, come friend, come confessor and yet all the time she was the most beautiful girl in town, and being Greek that was very hard for me to ignore!

"Do your family miss you?" I asked.

"Definitely," she answered straight away. "Who wouldn't miss me?" she added with mischief in her voice. "Seriously, though, I'm the youngest of four girls and so Ma is kept busy with all the Grand-childer back home. She writes to me every week, bless her, and gives me all the news from home. Da died a couple of years back…"

"I'm sorry to hear that," I mumbled.

"No need to be. It wasn't your fault. He was well into his sixties and smoked liked a chimney, so he did well to get that far. But it's hard on Ma being alone." Her mind drifted off across the world.

"I'm adopted," I said with an ease that amazed me. "But my Mum and Dad are the best people in the world, present company excepted."

Sue squeezed my arm. "And here's me thinking that the Irish lads were the biggest rogues on the planet."

"You obviously haven't met too many Greeks!" I retorted. We walked along in silence, passing the occasional duck squawking its displeasure at being disturbed from its evening forage. "But I think I'd like to know who my real parents were. Do you think that's a bad thing? And I've no idea how to find out without upsetting Mum and Dad." We walked on, and in the silence I became aware of the water lapping against the foreshore wall.

"I suppose it's one of those cases where you're damned if you do and you're damned if you don't." This time as she squeezed my arm she leaned her head against my shoulder, just for a second, and the scent of perfume paralysed my thoughts completely. I veritably bathed in the sound of the lapping water and the soft sounds of our footsteps on the grassy lawn.

"Do you have a boyfriend?" I asked in all innocence.

"Of course," she replied coquettishly. "And why wouldn't I?" Her eyes flashed at me in the evening light. "The trouble is that he's in Ireland. He's hoping to get his work visa in the next few weeks, so hopefully he'll be here by the end of next month."

"I'm really happy for you, Sue," I said, in a voice that bravely tried to hide my disappointment. As if trying to fill a deep hole that had suddenly appeared in my life, I suggested, "Maybe we could go camping down along the bends when he gets here."

"Maybe we could go before he gets here," Sue replied, while not changing pace and keeping her eyes firmly focused in front of her.

In an instant, a rocket-load of teenage romantic passion burst out of that deep hole and exploded into my universe. I didn't have a clue what to say.

"Sure thing," was my pathetic reply. "I think I ought to be getting home. Mum will have tea on the table." Inside I was screaming at myself at my weak-kneed approach to chatting up the mostly beautiful girl I'd met and who was offering to spend the night alone with me in a tent! What a loser I must've appeared to be!

"Grand," Sue said, "you mustn't keep your Ma waiting. But let me know if you'd like me to come camping with you."

"Of course I'd like it," I blurted out. "But how can I contact you? Where do you live?" Geez, I thought, my ancestors must be turning in their graves at my approach.

"I come here most evening about this time," she replied, "so maybe we can meet here and arrange the details." As an afterthought, she said, "But don't go getting any silly ideas about it, Tel, we'll be going camping as friends OK? Nothing more, so don't get your hopes up."

All I could do was smile foolishly back at her.

Naturally, for the next several days I stalked the foreshore each evening but without any sign of Sue. I even took a detour past the hospital hoping to get a glimpse of her. Then one evening, Sue was there, and I instantly forgot all my past frustrations.

"How are ye, Tel?" she greeted me, giving me a peck on the cheek.

"Good," was my well-rehearsed, highly insightful reply! I silently kicked myself up the backside. "So how's the life-saving business? Has Alexander Fleming shared his secrets about penicillin with you yet?" I discerned a decided lift in my dating game.

"Nothing so trivial," she answered, ignoring my comments. "One of your water sports colleagues came in, though. He'd water-skied into one of those dead trees in the lake. He said he thought that he had a splinter in his leg." She visibly winced as she spoke. "He wasn't joking either. The splinter was as big as my arm and about this long." She indicated the distance from her finger tips to her elbow. Now it was my time to wince.

"Ouch," I said, "that must have hurt."

"Actually, he wasn't in too much pain. But the whole thing was far too complicated for us to deal with it. Had to send him to the Base Hospital." She relived the incident in her mind. "He'll probably lose his leg, poor man." There's not much you can say to that.

"So, are we still on for camping?" My idea was that it would not only change the subject but also cheer her up, because she looked quite upset about the incident. Strike one to Tel the Greek.

Her eyes lit up and she linked her arm through mind as we retraced our steps along the foreshore. Soon we were in deep conversation planning who should bring what, where we'd meet and how long we should stay.

"I think you should know..." There was something in the way that she said it that made me stop walking and look directly at her. There was more than simple curiosity in my mind – there was a tinge of fear too. Was she going to bring a friend along with her? "My boyfriend is arriving in a couple of weeks. He's got his visa." The way she said it with such simple delight melted my inner despair and I think that deep within my mind I was really happy for her. But in another part of my mind, something shrivelled a little.

"That's exciting," I answered with barely concealed disappointment.

"The other good news is that I'm off this weekend, so we could go camping then." My rocket-ship of passion ignited its engines.

"I'll check with Mum and Dad and see if they can spare me from the shop. But I'm sure it'll be fine."

By the expression on her face I sensed that Sue knew more about the bonds of motherly love than I did.

"Let's meet here tomorrow and confirm everything's fine, eh?" With that we separated by the launch ramp, me going up Tiler Street and her going via Barrett Park to her digs somewhere near the hospital.

For some crazy, unfathomable reason, Mum smelled a rat. "You not like camping Telemachus. Bad for sleeping, too." Luckily for me she was cooking something on the stove and had her back to me.

The word 'but' was forming in my mouth …

"And think about the flies, and the mozzies, and the ants, if they don't eat you, snakes will," she concluded emphatically. "You need your sleep so you can study properly. It is important that you get your exams. You want to end up here stepping on rotten fruit all day or you want a decent job? Forget this nonsense, you stay home." She flashed her fish slice at me as if indicating that all argument was over.

I glanced at Dad. He silently shook his head to indicate that I should keep quiet.

Dad performed his usual magic. How he convinced Mum that camping would actually improve my studying technique remains a mystery to me. But, after all, the machinations of a Greek man's mind are why the Greeks have the monopoly on all the great stories in history.

Friday evening saw me carrying my swag and fishing pole out past the footy oval and heading out to the bends.

"G'day, Tel."

Kev's voice made me half jump out of my skin.

"G'day, Kev," I replied. "You frightened the life out of me."

"Hoping to catch something?" he asked with a knowing grin, suggesting that I had a sign on my head indicating to the world where I was going and what I was going to do. "Careful about what you catch down there, mate. A lot of people come back from fishing trips with more than just fish. See ya." With that, he headed back to town, it being the bewitching hour at the Royal Hotel.

I followed on down the track to a quieter camping spot near the ruins of the old saw mill, set my swag down and waited. Thankfully I didn't have to wait for long.

For an Irish girl, Sue seemed well prepared for camping out. "It does stop raining sometimes in the old country, you know," she said, as if she too could read my mind like an open book.

I ran my fingers through my hair as if rummaging for something. "Do I really have a sign up here that tells everyone what I'm thinking?" I asked, bewildered.

"Ah, Tel," she smiled, "as they say back home, you're as green as grass." And with that, she threw down her ruck-sack and pulled out her sleeping bag. Together we put up the tent and made the camp as comfortable as we could.

We had a glorious evening with doing nothing, yet sharing so much. She told me about Ireland, her family and her boyfriend Fachtna, from Cork, whose dad was a professor of something or other. Sue knew most of my history from my hospital sojourns, but something about the magic of the place melted my reserves and I shared my dreams about Ithaca. I was interrupted by the squawking of a mob of cockatoos high in the branches of a nearby river red gum. Their noise was followed by a deepening silence as the light fell away into the evening. In the moments that followed, stars appeared like silvered pinpricks in the rapidly darkening sky and a half-moon shone large over the edge of the trees while seemingly admiring itself in the waters of the river. Then I heard that haunting sound again.

"Was that an owl or a dog?" Sue asked.

"Both, really," I replied, feeling a little smug. "It's actually called a barking owl." Although there aren't as many around these days, it was one of the few night birds I knew and, call me quirky, but I'd always had a soft spot for owls.

"My Aunt Maeve had one get caught in her hair when I was a little child," Sue said quietly. "I've never felt comfortable about them since."

"That was probably a bat. Owls couldn't give a hoot about humans."

Sue groaned and smiled at the same time. "That's a terrible joke, Tel."

There was something so easy in her manner that I went on, "Did you know that in Greek mythology, the owl is associated with the goddess Athene? She was the friend of Odysseus, the father of Telemachus. Remember those dreams I told you about, well Athene actually told me that I didn't really have epilepsy and that I'd be OK to stop my meds." The words left my lips as naturally as if I'd just exchanged a pleasant g'day with a customer!

"You just gave me another reason to not feel comfortable about owls," Sue said lightly. The echo of the owl call faded, leaving only the mystical sound of the river running its course.

"I'm hungry," she said, getting up and rummaging in her backpack next to where we'd pitched the tent. She had her back towards me, which allowed me a moment to admire her taut frame.

"Are you still taking your tablets, Tel?" she asked matter-of-factly.

"Yeah," I answered, continuing to admire the scene before me. "I thought I should keep on taking them until I can work out how to get tested again. What do you think?"

"Sounds reasonable to me," she replied, "but then, I'm not a doctor, am I?" She turned and there was genuine empathy writ large on her pretty face. "Maybe you should ask your friend Mr O'Ryan about that. He's a terrible scallywag but I like the man. Mind you, I wouldn't trust him near mi' Ma, they tell me the man's dynamite with the older ladies!"

"Sue," I said in mock astonishment. "I'm surprised about you thinking such thoughts about Kev. Butter wouldn't…" But before I could finish, we'd both dissolved in fits of laughter.

As the moon cast its milky light over the camp, we lit a small fire in the fire pit left behind by previous campers. There was no wind and no fire restrictions – I was a stickler for fire safety. If you've ever experienced an out of control bush fire in Australia, then you'd know that it's worse than hell on wheels.

We ate some of the food that Mum had prepared for me. "There's enough here to feed a small army, Tel. Your mum must think you're going away for a month!"

"I can see that you've never eaten in a Greek house before. Perhaps we could change that," I quietly suggested.

"I don't think so, Tel. When Fachtna gets here I think he might not like me hanging out too much with the best-looking boy in town." I took that as a compliment, but it didn't feel like one.

I don't know how long we talked for. The night sounds and the flickering, glowing fire seemed to neuter the power of time. Then one yawn began to catch another and we decided that it was time to sleep.

If you've never met a good Irish girl you won't understand how beautifully innocent they seem to be, almost determinedly good! While I had one part of my brain pumping out hormones like there was no tomorrow, another part of me accepted this beautiful friendship as something pure and wonderful. Thankfully, Sue was strong for both of us and kept me on the right side of the fence.

It was a cosy two-man tent, and after I'd attended to the fire, we both settled into our separate sleeping bags. Sue had slipped into an oversized, black tee-shirt. "It's Fachtna's," she said.

Surprisingly, we fell asleep quickly and soundly.

The owl woke me during the night. As I lay listening to its haunting hoots, I quietly opened my sleeping bag and lay on top to feel the coolness in the air. Sue stirred from her sleep. "Are you awake, Tel?" she asked in the softest of voices.

"Sure am," I answered.

"Tel…"

"Yes?"

"Can I give you something?"

"Sure." Although the question sounded simple my heart jumped in my chest like a thoroughbred stallion.

"It's special." She spoke so low that it was hard to hear her clearly. But what sounded like a buzz-saw in my ears was the sound of her unzipping her sleeping bag.

"OK," I answered, with my heart now bouncing up and down in my throat.

"It's a memory that I'd like to give you. Our special secret." Saying that, she climbed out of her bag and set herself on top of me. All she was wearing was her black tee-shirt, but now she was so much closer, I could see the word Guinness across the front of it. I felt her breath on my face as her soft hair caressed my cheeks.

Enveloped in the silvered embrace of the moon's filtered light, something eternal and beautiful happened in that small tent. In that precious place, the two of us joined together, body, mind and soul. A liquid joy filled me, slowly coursing its way from my loins all through my body to find its lifelong resting place in a sacred place in my memory.

Afterwards, we lay enfolded in each other's arms, the top of her head tucked below my chin.

"Thank you," was all I could say.

Sue seemed to take a deep breath, and a slight pressure from her fingers on the back of my neck told me that she was happy too. Then we both slipped off into a deep, delightful sleep.

I got my wires crossed

"WAKE UP, SLEEPY head, I need a man to catch me some breakfast." Sue's head appeared through the flap of the tent.

"What time is it?" I asked dozily.

"Time you were up fishing," and she let go of the flap. I could smell smoke, so I assumed she must have been up for some time and set the fire again.

Pointing to the billy boiling over the fire she announced, "We nurses are handy people to have around, you know".

"I'm impressed," I replied in a muddled way. Sue was acting as if the most beautiful event in my whole life had just been a dream. "Sleep well?" I blurted.

"Like a log. You?" She stared across at me with her wide beautiful eyes.

"That was the best night of my life," I answered from the bottom of my heart.

"Great. Must be all this fresh air."

"Are you OK?" I inquired, taking a step towards her.

"And why wouldn't I be?" she replied with genuine ignorance.

"Just wondering," I said, buttoning up my shirt. "Sometimes the ground can be a little hard on soft bodies." I blushed as I uttered the words.

"We Irish are as tough as old boot leather when we need to be." She paused. "Are you feeling OK? You're not going to have a fit on me, are you?"

"I told you that I haven't got epilepsy anymore," I flashed back. I suppose it was a combination of resentment, confusion and being a teenager that caused my emotions to spin on a sixpence and spit out anger.

Sue was amazed. "Seems like someone got out of the wrong side of the sleeping bag this morning," she replied in a game attempt at humour, while poking a stick at the glowing embers.

"I'm sorry, Sue. It must be those bloody medications." I was thinking quickly on my feet. "I didn't mean to shout." The fire crackled and spat. The river flowed past, oblivious to everything in its path, while a duck swam regally at the head of its v-shaped wake. "I'll go and see if I can charm a fish onto my hook," I said, as hope struggled under the rubble of my memories.

I did get lucky and caught a small Murray cod. They're a beautiful fish to eat, and it didn't take long to clean it, scale it and skewer it on a rod over the hot fire. Its flesh began to sizzle and as the skin crisped, great globs of fish oil dropped into the heat, hissing their displeasure at coming to such an end.

"For a Greek greengrocer, you're a handy cook, Tel," Sue said. Relief swept over me as I felt the kindness in her voice.

"You're the kindest, most beautiful person I've ever met," was my heartfelt reply, but being young and not able to resist having the last word, "and you have the best collection of Guinness tee-shirts I've ever seen."

Sue's nose wrinkled a little and that troubled look flitted across her face. "Are you sure you're OK, Tel? What Guinness tee-shirt?" Immediately, a look of understanding washed over her features. "You mean the black one of Fachtna's that I had on last night. Don't let him hear you say that or he'll flatten you! He's a Cork man and hates Guinness – it's Murphy's stout for that man." She laughed. "And what is it with you young men? All you think about is beer and chasing girls."

Her laughter purified the atmosphere between us. Inside my thick skull, wheels were starting to turn, and with that motion came acceptance and understanding of the fragile tissue that separates truth from fiction and dreams from reality.

My brain had gone from clouded to confused, from doubt to enlightenment. It struck me that even if nothing had happened, if Sue hadn't been there then I wouldn't even have been able to have the most fantastic dream of my short life.

I grinned broadly. "Sue," I said, lifting the fish from above the flames and poking it to see if it was finished cooking, "you are the most delicious person I have ever met. This will have to count as the best fishing trip ever!" Looking up from the crisped cod I added, "And I mean that from the bottom of my heart."

"Well, thank you, kind sir," she answered, dropping a mildly mocking curtsey. "I must remember to take all my boyfriends fishing from now on if that's the effect it has on them." Her eyes flashed like sunlight on the ripples on a small pond.

The two of us sat on the banks of the river, well away from any rogue bull ants that might take a fancy to the fish or our flesh, and chatted idly as we finished our meal. By then, the heat was building with the advance of the day so we broke camp and headed back toward town.

"I'll wait here for a little while to give you a chance to head back on your own," I offered. "Can't go giving the local nurse a bad reputation by hanging out with a minor Greek god!"

"Who said you were a minor god?" she teased me back. Taking me by the finger tips, she embellished her farewell with, "I had a wonderful time, Tel. I'll always remember it. I hope you meet someone who truly deserves you." Then she leaned forward and kissed me lightly on the lips. Once more, I had a light-headed feeling.

"Good luck," I said feebly to her receding back. She turned one more time before disappearing around the bend and into the trees.

I hung around for about ten minutes doing God knows what. I thought about carving our names into a nearby river gum tree, but then I decided that was pretty stupid so instead I played soccer with a gumnut as I walked back along the path. I lost!

As the track opened out at the edge of the town, who did I bump into but KOR himself.

"G'day, Tel. Catch anything?" he asked with a mischievous smirk, which revealed his two rows of irregular teeth.

"Yeah, actually. I caught a pretty decent Murray cod and I don't mind if I say so myself, but I did a fairly good job of cooking it. Sue said…" In that instant, I suspect that I gave a wonderful impression of planting a size ten foot in my Greek mouth!

The good thing about Kev is that he doesn't labour the point – unlike most of my school mates who liked nothing better than teasing people until their ears incinerated.

"Nice girl, Sue," Kev said, blinking his eyes in his unique, owlish manner. "I hear the boyfriend is coming over from Ireland soon." He sniffed, causing the tip of his nose to veer towards his left cheek. "Shame, really," he mused. "What she needs is a good Aussie bloke to sort her out. Still," he paused while scanning the horizon for anything that he didn't know about already, "women can be tricky creatures. I'd stick to footy, if I were you. That way the only thing you might break is your leg. I'm off. See ya, Tel. You still OK to help out next week?"

"Sure thing, Kev. See ya." The man was way ahead of me.

Wrong time, wrong place

SOMETIMES COUNTRY LIFE can be a bit claustrophobic. Yeah, we have the biggest, bluest sky in the whole world, and yeah, the distant horizon is often obscured by a shimmering heat haze, but at the same time, everyone seems to know each other's business. So I wasn't particularly surprised when news spread of me and Sue going camping together. Strangely, I heard it back from an unusual source.

We had a new curate in town. Personally, I thought he was a good bloke but the majority of his flock thought him a bit of a 'dill'. He was about six-four in the old language and in terrible condition. He wore glasses and spoke with a plummy accent, despite the fact that he was born and bred in Bendigo, which wasn't his fault according to Kev! According to our new curate, "Leaving was the best thing I ever did," and that was all he would ever say on his past life.

Now, being a good Greek boy with good Greek parents, I definitely wasn't a Mick. But a good Greek Orthodox does make you stand out like a dog's fifth leg when you happen to be a student at the Convent of Mercy – or no-mercy, according to its adolescent inmates. As there was only one other Greek family in the district, there wasn't much call for ongoing Greek education in the area. The friendly teenage jibing between me and my Latin brothers rarely spilled into outright violence, but when it did, I liked to think that I acquitted myself with distinction!

Fr Bob was an ecumenical sort of bloke who'd studied in Rome, and as those Romans had nicked most of their culture from us Greeks, Dad and Mum always felt like he was more of a cousin than the enemy. So every now and then, Bob would appear at our back door and ask how the good Greeks were surviving the savages in the bush. Then he'd laugh raucously at his own humour. Mum would invite him in and give him a glass of wine before preparing a good feed for the man. Feeding a holy man was, for her, something akin to praying.

On those occasions, Bob would sit in his chair and share his wit and wisdom with me, as Dad was nearly always in the shop serving customers. Sometimes when Bob arrived, he looked shocking, as if he'd been up all night, which he often had been when keeping vigil over the dying required his eminent presence. "I'm buggered," he'd say when Mum wasn't listening, and in the blink of an eye he'd fall asleep for a few minutes. When he woke, his lids would part, a slow grin would spread to his chubby cheeks and he'd say, "You know something, Tel? You can only sleep with your best friends," and then he'd laugh one of his laughs again.

But I liked Fr Bob. I suppose you'd have called him an academic really. He read widely and shared my love of the *Iliad* and the *Odyssey*. "It must have been very different living back in those times, Tel. Morality and culture were so different. Most Australians just wouldn't understand these days. They'd think the Greeks were primitive idiots. Yet look what they achieved with their culture, philosophy, architecture and their mathematics. What have we done? TV and footy," and he'd roll his eyes up towards heaven.

Sometimes, though, I hoped that heaven was busy elsewhere! I remember one time Bob was at our place for a barbecue. He had a second large glass of red in his hand when he turned to me and announced in a stage whisper, "In the old days, Tel, we used to shit outside and eat inside!" Then he roared uproariously, leaving me to blush to the roots of my hair as everyone present turned to see what was going on.

A week after my camping experience out at the bends, Fr Bob heaved into view through the flywire of our open back door.

"Good evening, Tel," he boomed cheerily. "Mind if I come in?"

Without waiting for a reply, the squeak of the hinges informed me that he was coming in anyway. "Mind if I sit down?" he asked, flopping down once again before I had any opportunity to enter the conversation.

"Mum's in the kitchen."

"And what a fine job she does there too, Tel," he said.

"Good afternoon, Father." Mum had appeared. Nothing much gets past that woman's attention. "You like food?"

"Don't mind if I do. Thank you, Mrs A. I wouldn't mind a glass of that nice red, too, if there's any going spare. I've just been at the old people's home and it's an uncomfortable reminder of where I'm rapidly approaching. They're all sitting there with their mouths open catching flies!"

Sometimes Fr Bob could sound really cruel, but in fact that was his way of coping with aspects of intimacy that he felt uncomfortable with. "But you know what, Tel? I said Mass for the poor buggers. They wouldn't even know where they were, but when it came to saying the Our Father or the Hail Mary, they were word perfect! Amazing, isn't it?"

He scratched his curly black hair, which was heavily flecked with grey. He took his glasses off to polish them, a simple act that altered his appearance dramatically, before observing, "It's not an easy thing to do, Tel. Growing old gracefully, I mean." Replacing his glasses and wrinkling his nose he leaned in toward me, conspiratorially saying "In a certain sense I sometimes think we should grow old disgracefully, eh? What do you think?"

He paused for a second before laughing loudly at my discomfort.

"Taking of disgraceful, Tel," he said looking at me over the top of his glasses with a professorial sort of look, "I hear that a young man of my flock may have indulged in one of those dreadful sins of the flesh."

The word 'dreadful' dripped with dry, sarcastic wit, but the sentence hovered over my conscience like the sword of Damocles. Even though a thousand demon thoughts attempted to rush into my mind, they were frozen by the power of my embarrassment. Fr Bob held up his hand.

"Look, Tel," he said in a kindly voice, "if I believed half the things I hear, then this place would make Sodom and Gomorrah seem like a kindergarten! Mind you, I hope the good folk of this town only believe half the stuff they hear about me, too," and he laughed raucously again, slapping his knees to emphasise his delight!

"I have not the slightest interest in the goings on of the youth of this town – good luck to 'em, I say. They're no worse and no better than any generation that's gone before them and unlikely to be better or worse than the generations to come. But just be aware that we all have to accept the responsibilities of our actions and if you can do that, fair play.

"Oh, my goodness, Mrs A, you have prepared a feast fit for a ravenous curate! My, that looks good."

He picked up a chicken wing from the piled up plate she had brought in and chewed on it. He shot me a glance that suggested that his mission had been accomplished and that if I wished to, then I could escape now.

"I'll go and see if Dad needs a hand in the shop, Mum," I offered, but she was too busy bringing in more food to feed the holy man to reply, allowing me to slip out after giving Fr Bob a wink of acknowledgment.

I wondered how Father could have heard about my weekend so quickly, and then a thought struck me like a thunderbolt: if he knows, then who else knows? Does Dad know?

I stood in the doorway of the shop and watched Dad as he graded a recently arrived batch of tomatoes, tossing the occasional rotten one into a bin destined for the pig farm. Looking at his slight frame, I thought I sensed a slight bowing of his body, as if he was getting old. He worked such long hours and yet was always polite and helpful to anyone and everyone. I realised how much I loved the man, a feeling that only accentuated my guilt over the idea of seeking out my natural father. No man could hold a candle to my dad, and yet ...

"G'day, Tel," he turned and said. "How's Fr Bob? Still as erudite as ever? He should have been a professor in some smart university and not a curate in a dusty forgotten country parish. His brain's too big for his own good!"

"He's good, Dad. Mum's giving him a feed. I don't reckon he gets much to eat in the presbytery. I think the parish priest gets first dibs and makes Bob eat what's left over in the kitchen by himself. Need a hand with anything?"

"No, it's all good here, Tel. Quiet day today. Mondays usually are."

"OK if I go down to the foreshore and kick the footy around with the lads?"

"Have you taken your meds today?" he asked, while polishing a tomato to hide his natural concern for me.

"Absolutely," I answered, although since my last 'event' as I called it, I hadn't taken anything. "I'll be back in a couple of hours, if that's alright with you."

"Sure thing, Tel. Take it easy," and he gave me a sunny smile.

For some reason I felt impelled to go over to him and give him a hug. "Love you, Dad," I said.

"I love you too, son," he replied happily. "I love you very much."

I found the boys down on the foreshore playing footy and joined in. Within half an hour we were pretty spent so Yabby Mullins invited us to his place for a barbecue. "Picked some mushies this morning and they're delicious," he said.

"Whaddya know about mushrooms, Yabby? You been lookin' for the fairies underneath 'em, eh?" Goggs was a bit of a smartarse in a funny sort of way. Yabby was a good bloke, if a little simple, but he was brilliant at footy. Something to do with his long lanky frame and his long skinny arms. He'd catch a ball way higher than anyone else. He was Italian with jet black hair and a long pointy nose like his old man, all of which accounted for him being called Yabby.

"Someone go down to the bakery to pick up a couple of dozen rolls," said Yabby. "I'll fire up the barbie, drop on a few snags and then add these fresh mushrooms and we'll feast like kings."

"Are you sure you know which mushrooms to pick?" I inquired.

"Been doing it with my poppa for years and he's an expert. No worries, Tel. It's all good," he reassured me. And he was as good as his word. Within half an hour we were sitting on the wall outside of his house and feasting on our sausage and mushroom rolls.

"Anyone got the time?" Goggs asked.

"If you've got the inclination," came the swift riposte, which was rapidly followed by deep groans and calls of 'give it up, Dave'.

"It's about six o'clock," someone offered.

"Damn," I mumbled, having jammed the bun in my mouth while pulling my shirt over my head. "I've gotta get back to help Dad shut up shop. Thanks for the barbie, Yabby," and I set off up Moat Street at a canter.

Just as I got to the corner of Moat and Macquarie Streets, my world went very foggy and my stomach felt like it was made of rubber. Flashes of light illuminated my vision before a falling sensation took over, and I felt like I was being sucked into the middle of the earth. I remember slumping to the ground as sweat poured out of every pore in my body. The last thing I saw was the outline of a dark head coming into sight before everything went black.

When I opened my eyes the black head was still there, but there was also the firm pressure of someone's hand gripping my shoulder.

"Are you alright, boy?" a voice was saying.

I held up my arm to shield me from the bright sunlight that was pouring through an open window. "What happened?" I asked. I licked my lips, which were parched dry.

"Forgive me," the voice of old Laertes said, "I should have woken you earlier. Even in the early morning, it can get very hot in summer here in Ithaca."

I let out a groan. Not again! I shifted slightly and the old man came into view. "I thought it was the mushrooms," I said weakly. "Yabby..." I began, but then gave up trying to explain. "Any news?" I asked instead.

"We have some food for you. Mentor tells me that your journey has been long and challenging. May the gods bless you and wise Athene keep you safe. Come," he ordered, heading outside.

Before rising I checked my trousers. Not a sign of urine, which made me smile. "You owe me, Yabby," I muttered under my breath.

Outside, there was a spread on an old wooden table in the shade of a vine-covered pergola. Mentor was sitting on a low stool dipping rough bread into a surprisingly delicately-crafted wooden bowl, which contained some sort of broth. His gaze drifted lightly across the scene before his eyes. Cleaning his fingers on his short tunic, he said, "How often do we fail to see something when it's right there before our very eyes?" I followed his gaze, trying and failing to see what he'd seen.

To me it all looked and sounded very normal: bushes, trees, sand and the sound of birds tweeting! Mind you, it was a cracker of a day and a lot like back in Yarramah, but with more rocks and hills.

"Over there in that bush." He pointed to a dense, prickly bush about ten yards away. I stared hard. After several seconds I noticed that I was holding my breath. "Nope, nothing," I said, releasing the pent-up air.

"Patience."

Suddenly I saw a flash of blue. Its brilliance brashly defied the surrounding ordinariness. The small wren-like bird with its cocky, proud tail twisted boldly on a small branch.

"Wow. That's so beautiful," I whispered to Mentor. We both sat in silence as if our combined power of thought would hold it there for as long as possible. It was a deep and precious moment. Then my impetuosity drove me to get a better look, and with one small step, the magic ceased and the bird took flight. "It looked like a willie wagtail, but so much more beautiful. I've never seen anything like that before. What do you call them Mentor?"

"A sign from the gods."

The birds sang from the treetops and a soft breeze blew in from the sea, caressing our faces. "I think they are blessing us."

Such thoughts had never really crossed my mind. It seemed that several years of Catholic education had failed to have much of an impact on the spiritual side of my nature. Fr Bob used to go on about Christ and things, and to some extent I could get the Jesus bit. JC was a decent enough sort of bloke who did the right thing. I could even get miracles: if you'd seen my mum cook for a crowd of hungry Greeks, you'd definitely understand the loaves and fishes one. But God and gods and spirits? It was all too elusive for my brain.

"All I saw was a beautiful bird, Mentor. How come you think it was the gods?" I asked with genuine sincerity.

The dear man dipped his bread once more and tore off a decent sized chunk before chewing on it. For him the silence brought comfort, but for me it brought frustration. Perhaps there was a message in that, too.

"Why did you need to move closer?" he challenged me between chews.

"I only wanted to get a better look at it," I pleaded like a spoiled child.

"Would you agree that it was your impatience that drove its beauty from your sight?" He stopped to clear a chunk of recalcitrant bread from between his front teeth. "Thus it is with the gods. They come to those who are present and patient. But they only approach when and where they are ready."

A flash of blue light sped from the thorn bush and disappeared.

"You are blessed indeed," Mentor said to me with a wry grin, "and so am I."

I felt there was too much mystical stuff going on here so I decided to change the course of the conversation and steer it toward more solid ground.

"Laertes seems a nice man. I'd always thought that he was a pretty grumpy bloke." Mentor looked at me quizzically. I realised that I had suffered an exacerbation of my foot in mouth disease! "I mean, that's what the blokes on the boat said. They reckoned that it was probably because he was so grumpy that Odysseus stayed away for so long. Seems like the old man was a fairly tough task master."

Mentor studied the grain of his wooden eating bowl.

"The relationship between father and son is an ever-evolving one." He dipped his last remaining bread in his broth and soaked up the remnants. It appeared that Mentor loved the silence between speaking just as much as he enjoyed sharing his wisdom. "Remember, every father was a son once."

"Do you have any children, Mentor?" The sentence was carried away by the soft breeze but no answer replaced it. "My dad is the kindest person I know," I began, but forming the next word was proving harder than I'd expected. The sun was rising in the sky and with it the intensity of heat increased, too. Although I'd thought that Ithaca was similar to Australia, now I was beginning to notice the differences. The sky looked as blue but seemed smaller and hazier. Insight can be a strange thing, especially for young people.

"He's not my real dad, though," I finished. "I wish to God he were." I looked at Mentor, who, to my discomfort, had been watching me closely. "Do you think it wrong that I should try to discover who my real father is, Mentor?"

The decent man held my gaze, studying my face. "You are troubled by seeking the truth, and that can be a good thing, young friend of Telemachus. Sometimes truth can be more damaging than lies. Truth can destroy a man's reputation, but in the end truth is a far more certain foundation on which to build one's life. But always remember that truth can be a double-edged sword. You must respect it and be prepared to live with its consequences."

"But how do you know what the truth is?" A sense of frustration had been building as I listened to him. It always seemed to be so unjust to young people to always be hounded with expressions like 'tell the truth, or else...' The 'truth' was used like a cudgel to bludgeon us into submission or mindless servitude.

"Who decides what the truth is, Mentor?" I challenged him. "Is it the person with the greatest power or the person with the most powerful words?"

Instead of reacting to my barely veiled antagonism, my old friend shrugged his shoulders under his well-worn cloak. "I wish I knew," was all he said. "I believe that the line of truth and honesty passes through each man's heart, and a man's heart can be a mystery even to the man himself."

The sound of old Laertes cutting down more thorn branches came to us from the other side of the small dwelling.

"He's a tough old man," Mentor said, nodding his head in the direction from whence the sounds were coming. "I've no doubt he would rather be gentler and kinder, but life fashions us to her needs. Odysseus was not an easy child." He smiled as if remembering something from long ago. "Many's the time old Laertes had to pull his son into line and many's the time Odysseus rebelled against such seemingly stifling parenting. You see, most fathers set standards for their sons which they themselves learned from their own fathers. A few, the wiser ones, keep the more creative ideas while discarding the damaging ones. And a few even add some new ideas of their own – some good, some not so good. Laertes was a wise father, although I am certain that Odysseus would have challenged that notion when he was a youth."

I felt myself becoming uncomfortable. My dad was just a great dad, and yet he wasn't even my dad – my real dad had abandoned me! Believe me, that's a very schizophrenic feeling! Some of my mates at school had far different relationships with their fathers, mostly good, but some were downright destructive.

"It seems to me," I began, attempting to fashion my words into some sort of coherent conversation, "that most teenagers resent their dad, but when they get to be a dad themselves, they resent the way in which their own sons seem to abandon them like an old pair of socks."

Mentor gave me one of those KOR looks – the one where he looks like a super intelligent chicken staring at you sideways. "You have a wise head on young shoulders, young Telemachus. Yet on Ithaca, most young men are taught to respect their father even if they disagree with them. It is instilled from infancy that their fathers are worthy of such respect and that one day they too will assume their own responsibilities. It is important that they learn from the examples of their own fathers."

In a flash, the little blue bird reappeared in the bush and we fell silent, looking on in quiet awe. It leaped from twig to twig, performing a feathered version of Charlie Chaplin and finished off with a flamboyant wag of its obsidian tail. We marvelled at its colourful cameo. To our delight, it flew to the ground and landed just in front of us, twitching its tail from side to side and fixing its coal-black eye first on Mentor and then on me. Then, in an instant, it was gone.

"The gods are never far away." My friend smiled at the empty stage. "And they remind us of the frailty of beauty and the passing nature of pleasure."

I got up and leaned against one of the wooden pergola posts. It shifted slightly under my weight. My mind was shifting too, shifting to how Odysseus could be gone for twenty years and then turn up expecting everything to be hunky dory. How could that happen in real life? Why had all these people waited for him so loyally and then carried on as if nothing had happened? If my dad didn't turn up in time for tea, there would be hell to pay from Mum!

"I don't get it, Mentor," I said, speaking my thoughts aloud. "How come Odysseus is such a hero when he abandons his family and then expects everyone to welcome him back like the hero he'd been at Troy all those years ago?"

As my emotional squall abated, the breezes whispered their secret thoughts to the dried grasses which bordered the nearby track.

"Only winners use the term 'hero'," Mentor sighed, "but they have a very narrow vision of the world." Pushing his bowl away from him, he added with a smirk, "You should have had some of that, it was delicious!"

He picked the husk of a nut from between his front teeth before continuing. "When Telemachus was a child, he suffered greatly at the loss of his father. As did Penelope. She grieved behind closed doors, afraid to let her worst fears infect the servants and shepherds lest they abandon her. But Telemachus lacked the guile to hide his hurts. I did my best and walked with him as he gathered wood for the home fires. He didn't say much. How could he? He didn't know how. But I heard him sobbing with his mother most nights when dreams disturbed his sleep and he woke in fear.

He was a long time understanding the meaning of his loss and the wound it had caused."

"What happened?" I asked naively.

Dear Mentor allowed himself a brief chuckle. "A slave saved him," he said, his creased face turning to me and smiling. "Telemachus was out with Eumaeus one day, watching over the pigs. Eumaeus had returned to his hut to get some water and dainties for them both. He is a kind and good man and looked on Telemachus as a much-loved son. A slave from Ethiopia was passing along the road. 'What news?' shouted young Telemachus, as the man appeared to be walking past without acknowledging him. The tall man paused and turned in the young lad's direction. 'I have news to suit your every mood, young master. What would you desire?'

"Now, Telemachus sought only news of his father and answered, 'I seek news of my father, proud Odysseus who fought in the Trojan wars these many years past.' 'I have heard of this man,' the Ethiopian replied. Odysseus is a man of great renown and many stories are told of his great deeds even in the distant lands from whence I come. But not for some years had I had any news of your father."

"The news did nothing to improve Telemachus' mood. He picked up a stone and threw it at the man as one might throw a stone at a stray dog to scare it away. It struck the man on the forehead, causing him to fall to the ground. Filled with remorse, young Telemachus ran over to him and lifted him from the dust. He beseeched forgiveness from the slave and used his own shirt to help staunch the flow of blood from the Ethiopian's wound. It was then that he realised that the man was blind, which only deepened the horror at his own impetuous outburst.

"All the while, the slave never stopped smiling. He asked Telemachus why he was so aggrieved, after all, he himself was just a slave and Telemachus obviously a man of great standing. The boy had no answer, only deep remorse. The slave told him that often it is the unintended wound inflicted by another that binds us closer together. All that is needed is forgiveness, which he offered to Telemachus with genuine freedom.

"Wounds, forgiveness, freedom, love – they all come from the same source," Mentor said. "Every good father comes to learn these things, though it takes their sons many years to discover this truth.

"Telemachus took the man into his own household, where he had a place of high esteem at table. Then one day he was gone. No-one knew where. Some said he was a god come down to teach Telemachus wisdom, others that he was a charlatan who stole the affection of a naive young man and ran off with some treasure. So many stories were told, but Telemachus himself never listened to them. He knew that it was he who had received the great gifts of wisdom and friendship from a stranger, and in his own heart he wished his friend well wherever he was."

There was so much said in that short conversation that I felt the need to be by myself in order to absorb all that I had heard. Mentor knew that. Standing up from his stool, he stretched and then pointed in the direction of some birds circling in the distance.

"Ithaca," he said simply. "The seagulls think it is an earthly paradise with all the waste that we men drop to the ground. If you keep them in sight as you walk, you will be at the house of Odysseus before the sun reaches its zenith. Here, take this with you," and he handed me a half-full wineskin, "it can get hot out on the track. Stick to the path and you won't get lost. Tell the servant at the door to take you to meet Penelope immediately."

It was what he didn't say next which made me look at him. Was there another mystery there that I didn't know about?

"Thanks, Mentor. Will you be coming into town as well?"

"I will attend old Laertes and then perhaps we will join you. I suspect that we will all be needed there before too long." I returned his knowing look in spades, being in the advantageous position of having read the book already!

As I walked along, my mind was full of firefly thoughts that flashed in and out of my consciousness. In fact, I missed the first part of the journey as thought after thought distracted my attention.

Stubbing your toe against a rock has a powerful way of bringing your mind into the present. In an instant I was hopping on one leg and watching as blood oozed from the graze on the end of my big toe. If Mum had been there, I would have been in all sorts of trouble because I filled the air with foul imprecations of a most imaginative kind.

Paradoxically, the rest of the walk became much easier as all I had to do was focus on my pain while making sure that I avoided any more killer rocks. Suddenly my mind just had one, solitary focus.

At one point I sat on a boulder in the shade of a limestone cliff to rest my foot. The pain was subsiding and the blood had coagulated, making the injury look far worse than it no doubt was. As I sat there holding my injured foot up on my other leg, I took the time to look around me. You couldn't say the countryside was beautiful – it was dry and dusty; the bushes were scrubby and coated with vicious thorns. Ants of various denominations marched in straight lines, pausing in the shadow of my leg to work out a new route, while the bigger ones threatened to climb up and get a taste of my blood. These I flicked away with a stick that lay close by.

I was having fun flicking those ants – it was real David and Goliath stuff, but on this occasion the big guy was winning.

While prosecuting this pyrrhic battle, I failed to notice a whole community of ants whose home the boulder was, the most ferocious of which began to appear in my peripheral vision. When they started to test the thickness of my shorts with their evil-looking mandibles, I decided to decamp and leave them to it. Between the stubbed toe and the intractable arthropods, my mind had become very much focused in the present.

The cicadas wove their piercing music from a myriad of branches, and every now and then something scurried off into the undergrowth: lizards probably. I wasn't worried about snakes, they're dopier creatures when it's hot, unless you happen to stand on one! Mostly they just coil up in the sunshine to soak up the rays, and when they do deign to move, they're really quiet, which is why they're so successful at what they do.

I reached the edge of the settlement, where I was met by sleepy dogs who merely raised their weary heads in the shade of low bushes. One crusty canine did manage to conjure up a grumbling growl before deciding it was too hot to bother. I made for the walled compound, home to Telemachus and Penelope.

To the son of a Greek expat, it all looked very familiar. From time to time, Mum and Dad used to get postcards from back home with pictures of places like this on them. By the main entrance of Odysseus' home, an old olive tree gave shelter to one of the servants. I went over to him and began to explain who I was, but he remembered me from the last time. That didn't stop him from giving me a somewhat contemptuous look before letting me past. Perhaps he thought his suspicions were right and that in fact I really was one of those suitors who'd been plaguing Penelope ever since Odysseus had gone missing in action.

Inside the place looked like party central.

Some of the suitors were sitting around the table talking, while others were shouting at each other as if they were about to start a fight. Scraps of food littered the table, the floor and even the walls! Wineskins, fresh and old, lay on the table. An old dog lay in the corner with one eye open, watching the whole procedure with ancient disdain; I smiled as I recognised my old friend Argos. He caught sight of me looking at him and the hackles briefly rose on the back of his neck. Even from where I was standing I could hear the rumble of his growl. Then he stopped. He held my gaze for a few moments, and in that time, I swear he winked at me. That dog was all class! Having completed his cameo performance, he wagged his tail once before closing his white rimmed eyes and resuming his doggy doze.

"You made it." It was Telemachus who spoke. He'd come up behind me out of the shadows of the cloister. "How was old Laertes when you left him? Does he know of my father's return?"

"He's good," I replied. "A bit grumpy, but hey, if I'd disappeared for twenty years without telling my old man where I'd gone, I reckon he'd be pretty miffed too." For all his severe exterior, my friend had a decent sense of humour, too.

"My mother is expecting you. Come." With that, we left the noise of the interlopers and headed to the room where

Penelope had lived for all those years, to where she used her guile and her weaving to keep the suitors at bay until such time as her beloved would return.

In a quiet corridor away from the dining hall, we passed an old maid carrying a bundle of sheets. She eyed us with a crone's eye while spearing Telemachus with a questioning look. No words were spoken. As we approached Penelope's rooms, Telemachus whispered, "That was Eurycleia, my old nurse. She's been in this house since my father built it. She knows all our secrets," he looked at me before adding, "and all our weaknesses too."

"Can she turn children into toads?" I mocked back. But from the look on his face, I knew that I'd insulted someone special.

"What she lacks for beauty on the outside she more than makes up for on the inside." I felt duly smacked between the eyes – metaphorically speaking.

My friend stood before a heavy wooden door and knocked twice. A muffled voice could be heard from the other side. Telemachus opened the door and entered, and I followed behind. He greeted his mother and whispered a few words in her ear. She inclined her head as if agreeing to something.

"I have some matters to attend to with the suitors," he said, turning to me. "I'm sure Mother will keep you entertained." He grasped me by my wrist in the Greek fashion, and I grasped his in return. His grip was powerful despite his youth. I reckon he'd make a half decent cricket player back home.

The room we stood in was light and airy. There was not a man's touch to be found anywhere. On a small altar there were symbols of the goddess Athene, and lingering in the air was the strong scent of rosemary. Penelope saw me look at the altar. "Athene has long been our shelter in times of need but we must be patient, the gods come and go at their own time and place."

Geez, I thought to myself, this woman was a supremely patient lady. She'd been waiting over twenty years for her old man to come home and yet her only sign of hope, seemingly, was the smell of an old herb bush! Still, that's Greek women for you. Mum's just the same: she still thinks I'm going to be brain surgeon one day.

Two things stood out in her room: one was the amazing bed right in the middle – it was huge. The other was a loom that sat in the corner surrounded by threads of every weft and hue. Penelope saw me look at it.

"How much longer can I keep the suitors at bay?" she asked, almost to herself. I knew the answer to that question and something inside of me suggested that she thought I knew, too, but that it was a question that she couldn't or wouldn't ask me. Deep inside myself I'd already come to the conclusion that I was just an observer in this story and there was no way that I wanted to become a part of it. If I did, I stood a good chance of being stuck in history forever.

"You are a strong woman, my lady," I began, "and your people survive on the strength of your love for Odysseus. As it is with your gods, hope can be just as powerful as signs and wonders."

She looked at me, searching my face for something. "You are an unusual young man, Telemachus. And I thank you for your words." Once more the air went out of her hope, and her expression grew heavy with the burden of another day having to foist off the men who were threatening to take over her household and her life. Despite her natural beauty, the lines of suffering were to be seen around her eyes, which had seen so much, and around her mouth, which had held back so much pain for so many years. This good woman was intimately aware of the meaning of suffering, just as much as any great warrior who'd been into battle and been scarred by it.

"I hear there's another stranger in town," she said as she sat at her loom, quietly unpicking all the work she'd done that morning. From the story told to me by my father, I knew that she'd held off naming a new husband by saying that she wouldn't announce who she'd marry until she'd finished weaving this particular garment. And each evening she would unpick what she had woven that day. They say, "Beware of Greeks bearing gifts," but until you've dealt with a Greek woman, you know nothing about sleight of hand.

"I heard that rumour as well, my lady," I answered briefly, before biting my tongue into submission.

"You have learned discretion, Telemachus. You are an exceptional young man." She allowed the shadow of a smile to lift one side of her mouth, thus restoring her beauty in an instant.

There was a soft knock at the door. "Come," she said. The only sound that could be heard when the door opened was my chin hitting the floor. In walked a chimera of Julie and Sue. She immediately blushed when she saw me staring at her, which made Penelope's smile widen. The girl held a skein of fresh wool for her mistress, but I was entranced by her half-plaited hair, which tumbled beautifully down along one side of her delicious Greek neck. She was about the same build and height as Sue, but whereas Sue's skin was white, this girl's skin was brown. Yet it was her eyes that reminded me of Julie, without the contact lens effect. She was wearing a long pleated dress cinched tight at the waist with a beaded belt, such as you'd imagine a young goddess would wear.

"Thank you, Helen," Penelope said, "you may leave it here." The girl floated across the room before my eyes and placed the soft wool on a table next to her mistress.

"Will that be all, my lady?" The sound of her voice was like springtime, when all the sweetest of sounds are first formed. This was a moment for which all Greek men were made, to feel love course through their hearts, their minds and their bodies.

"That will be all," Penelope said, but from the way she spoke I had the strong feeling that the words were directed mainly at me! When my pretty vision had left the room, her mistress returned to her warp-weighted loom. Picking up a spindle, she began to wind the new skein onto it. "Helen is the niece of Eurycleia." I don't know why but the sentence had the effect of a cold bucket of water being thrown in my face. I'd only seen Eurycleia for a few moments but I reckon even Zeus would think twice before taking her on!

"Tell me what you know of the stranger," Penelope asked.

I told her what little I knew, that he was an old man who'd turned up, and that Eumaeus was looking after him. That as far as I knew he had no news of her husband. Her hand paused on the distaff. How many times had she been disappointed over the years, I wondered, and my heart ached for her. She was so close and yet it must have felt so far!

"Thank you, Telemachus. You may go now."

"Yes, my lady," I replied, bowing my head before turning to leave. I felt a real bastard and paused in the corridor, leaning back against the closed door, trying to regain my composure. As I turned to go and find Telemachus, I saw Eurycleia watching me from the far end of the passageway. It was like she was interrogating me without speaking. The woman terrified me.

I went back to where the suitors were making a feast for themselves and stood deep in the shadows, watching and listening. Of Telemachus there was no sign.

After a while it became apparent that the leader of them all was a man called Antinous. He was one of those short guys who made up for lack of stature with a mountain-sized ego and a bullying attitude. He was about five foot six in the old language, carrying a bit too much condition around his gut, and his black, cropped hair was already receding at the front, which made him look older than he probably was.

He was the sort of person that most reasonable people take an instant dislike to, but unfortunately he was also one of those people who seemed to attract weaker, sycophantic idiots to do their dirty work. He was rubbishing Telemachus, calling him weak and not fit to run the place now that Odysseus wasn't coming back. Basically, that there was no way the kid could organise the equivalent of an Aussie piss up in a brewery! I mumbled a word that rhymes with 'banker' under my breath, but obviously it was a bit louder than I intended.

"You, slave, come here. What did you say?" I looked in askance at him and pretended that I didn't understand. "He even employs fools and idiots to serve him at table." This was obviously very witty as it brought the house down with laughter from his mates, but I decided that discretion was the better part of valour and chose that moment to slink off into the shadows.

"It was not wise to bait Antinous, my friend." It was Mentor.

"How'd you get here?" I asked in genuine astonishment. He stared back at me and his eyes sparkled like a youth. From somewhere the scent of rosemary appeared and I understood.

"Our friend Antinous not only has a voracious appetite for what he can find at table, but he also craves powe. Yet what makes him a very dangerous man is his cruelty. He would have you roasted on a spit alive if the humour took him, and baste you with the wine from his own goblet. Do not cross him, else you won't live to regret it."

That was the trouble with short people with big egos, somehow they cornered the market in real nastiness and rightly needed to be feared. I began to think that if Kev had been here, the situation would have been somewhat different, but then another thought dawned upon me: perhaps he was.

"What's happening?" I asked. "Did Odysseus get his men together to get rid of this mob?"

"He has as many as he needs," Mentor replied.

"Oh, dear," I thought to myself, "this is going to get very messy." I couldn't remember what happened at the end of the Odyssey, but I did know it involved a great deal of killing – but who got killed and by whom, I couldn't remember!

"I have a message from Eurycleia." Now that did get my attention. I wasn't sure which was a worse fate: upsetting Antinous, or getting a dressing down from the old maid of the premises. "She awaits you at the back of the house." I was tempted to ask if I could borrow his sword, but it seemed a bit excessive so I decided against it.

Having received the directions, I made for my assignation with the ancient one not knowing whether to be terrified or just ... terrified. There was no door to the hut where I was to attend, but outside were white linen sheets strung out in the sunshine to dry. There were some old stone bowls, which I presumed was where the washing was done, and close by them were amphora where, if my sense of smell was correct, urine was stored. You've got to believe me, but I do know some Greek history and strangely enough, they didn't have washing machines way back then. Bowls were filled with water, clothes were added, young boys jumped up and down on them and then the urine was added to whiten it all! But don't suggest that to your mum if you want to keep your head on your shoulders.

As I was thinking about all this, Eurycleia came out of the shadows and began to walk down a path to a nearby stream. I didn't need to be told, I just followed until I was given further orders.

We came to the stream and she sat on a smooth rock that had obviously seen a thousand backsides in its time. She indicated that I sit next to her. When she spoke, she had an incredibly soft voice, which put me at ease immediately.

"You are not from Ithaca." It wasn't a question.

"Yes, Sister," I replied, as if I was in first grade and one of the nuns had just told me to sit still. It appeared that some parts of my Catholic education had stuck, mainly because they were associated with fear! Eurycleia ignored me.

"These are troubled times."

"Yes, Eurycleia".

The stream rolled its way through the well-worn rocks, flashing sunlight from its shimmering surface.

"Helen would like to meet you. She's over there." She pointed to an almond tree, the boughs of which brought shelter to the banks a short distance away. Helen looked so slender. My legs felt weak as I rose and walked towards her. Everything in the whole world seemed magnified: the colours, the sweet sounds, the freshness of the air and most of all, Helen herself.

"G'day," was all my great Greek intelligence could come up with for an intro.

"Greetings, Tel."

"You know my name?" I was incredulous and grinned appropriately.

The sun's light reflecting off the water danced around her, making it difficult to see her clearly. Then my head began to spin.

"Wow. You look like a real goddess," was all I managed to mutter before I slumped down on the bank at her feet.

Laughter like a thousand tiny bells filled the air.

"Oh, Tel," a voice said.

A plot hatched

THE LIGHT DANCED in my eyes. I held up my hand to block it out.

"What has my boy done now?"

That was no goddess speaking – except in Dad's eyes!

"This is all your fault!" Mum declared in her most intimidating voice as she half turned. Following her line of vision, I saw Yabby standing by the door of my room looking decidedly uncomfortable.

"Sorry, Tel. Must've picked one of the wrong 'uns." His voice trailed off.

Goggs, who'd loyally come in with his mate to face Mum's wrath, gave Yabby a tug on his sleeve. "Best we leave Tel to recover, eh?" Looking sheepishly toward me he added, "See you at footy training on Thursday, eh?"

Some of Mum's looks have been known to melt steel, and sensing such a stare coming in his direction, Goggs dragged his mate out through the door of my bedroom and vanished.

Mum was about to launch into one of her, "I told you about eating Italian food," when Doc Buckley's face appeared from under my bed.

"I dropped the thermometer," he said, grasping the silvered wand in his hand, his face flushed with the effort. Both his eyebrows threatened to tango with his hairline, such was the height they reached.

"It appears that you've had a profound case of ergot poisoning – not another epileptic fit." Noting my vacant expression he explained, "Ergot is a chemical which is found in some mushrooms. Ever since Adam was a lad, it's been known to cause hallucinations. It has a fascinating history." Pausing for theatrical effect, he added, "And I believe you were talking about a goddess just before you woke up."

My pupils must have dilated, causing the dear man to grin a grin that only a truly happy man can fashion.

"He should be alright now, Mrs A. Just keep him quiet for the rest of the day and call me if you have any problems." The man was all business now as he packed his bag and bustled out of the room.

Mum stood there looking at me. A tear formed in the corner of her right eye. She opened her mouth as if to say something, thought better of it, sniffed loudly and left. Soon I heard the sound of pans clattering in the kitchen and then

I knew that she was indulging herself in a bit of culinary therapy. The aroma of herbs and onions soon reached me.

"What's for tea, Mum?" I shouted.

"Spanakopita," she shouted back.

"Yum."

I could hear Dad bustle into the kitchen. The pans paused their clattering for a moment before the sound of chair legs scraping along the tiled floor broke the silence. That was Dad again. He always dragged the chair away from the kitchen table before slumping down into it after a long day's work. I could imagine the scene as he ran his hand through his salt and pepper hair, in relief at what he'd just heard.

"Dad?"

"Yes, son."

"Any watermelon in the shop? Mi' mouth's as dry as the inside of a cockie's cage." I knew that would make him smile.

"I'll get some for you." This time the chair almost sang with his happiness as he got up straight away and went back out to the shop.

"Who's helping Dad, Mum?"

"Kath came down as soon as she hear you sick again."

"Good ol' Kath," I said, more to myself than to Mum. For a big lady who smoked too much, Kath had a heart as big as a Ford F100 truck. Thinking about Kath turned my mind to Kev. Him and Mentor ... they were too alike for it to be just a coincidence. But somehow I just couldn't get my head around the idea that there were crazy gods wandering around either trying to help out or cause trouble. Although, when you looked at the world, it really was a pretty crazy place.

After tea I asked Mum if it was ok for me to go for a quiet walk down Lisle Street and back. As Goggs said about his parents, "It's always best to get your retaliation in first." Mum looked at me as if she were judging the ripeness of a pomegranate. She glanced at my empty plate which re-assured her.

"Don't be long," she said, "and don't eat no more of that Italian food, OK?"

"I might pop in and see Kev if he's still at the cement works," I proffered from the doorway, "The Royal doesn't open for another half hour so I might just catch him."

"Don't let that man play with your head, and be back soon. All this drama, it send me to an early grave."

"No, Mum. Yes, Mum. Sorry, Mum."

It was still a cracker of a day outside and the sidewalk along the street was dotted with people who'd just stopped to have a yarn with one another. A steady stream of mums were heading in and out of the main store with various it-erations of children dragging, or being dragged behind them. Old Mr Kelly was outside of his business watch-ing the world go by, as he'd done for the last seventy-odd years. No-one knew how old he was: probably well over eighty, but his mind was still as sharp as a butcher's knife.

"G'day, Tel."

"G'day, Mr Kelly."

"You OK now, Tel?"

"Fit as a mallee bull, Mr Kelly."

He snickered a little. "Just make sure you don't end up in the knackers yard like the rest of those flamin' bulls, young lad!"

It was my turn to snicker. That man held more knowledge under his thinning, white pate than all of the people in the solicitors' office next door.

I heard the mixer, then the transistor radio before I heard the steady scraping of the trowel on the drying cement. Kev always finished a job neatly, even if he was under great pressure. "No point going off half-cocked if you're running a business," he'd say. I watched him until he'd finished. He picked up a bottle of water next to him and drained the last dregs. "G'day, Tel. Off mushrooming?"

"You should be on the stage Kev – sweeping it," I replied, with a fat grin on my face.

"Kev?"

"What?"

"Do you believe in God?"

His black eyebrows arched briefly. "I used to be an altar boy. Knew all the responses in Latin, too. Trouble is I also knew where Fr Mulroney kept the key for the altar wine. Apparently it's a mortal sin to drink wine. That's why I only drink beer now. Reckon that counts?"

"Seriously, Kev, do you ever think that there's something greater than us? You know, like..." I searched my brain for an appropriate example, "Why there are so many beautiful Greek women."

Kev dug the pointed end of his trowel into the pile of cement next to him as if it was a stiletto. "It seems to me that all that trying to work out if there's a god or there isn't a god is a complete waste of time. I love beer, it tastes bloody marvellous to me and don't ever try to come between me and a frosty glass of VB." There was a genuine menace in his voice.

"God knows how they make the stuff and at the end of the day who cares. If yer spend all your time working out how it got there, it'd be bloody warm by the time you got to drink it. Talking of which," he glanced up at the clock wired to a metal stanchion, "the pub'll be open soon."

"So you do believe in miracles then, sort of?"

The look he gave me ended that brief philosophical debate.

"Kev?"

"Bloody hell, Tel, you're enough to drive a man to an early grave with all these questions! What is it now?"

"Remember you said you'd help me find out about who my real parents were?"

"Correct," he fired back at me as his eyes assumed a black gimlet look.

"Well, can you help me?"

"For a start, you can give me a hand tidying up." He nodded in the direction of the broom. It was an invitation that needed no answer. He began washing out the cement mixer and when he was satisfied that it was as he wanted it, he flicked the switch, leaving only the transistor radio to report on the next day's horse races at Ballarat.

"My brother Tom has a hotel in Melbourne. Nice place. Tom's a good business man but loves the horses too much. Almost as much as he likes the ladies. A lot of the toffs go to Tom's place, civil servants and the like. I rang him after you talked to me. Said he'd ask around. Said there were some people that owed him. Tom's a good scout!"

I hosed down a section of the floor where wet concrete had spilled and gave it a vigorous brushing.

"Thanks, Kev. When do we go to Melbourne?"

"Bugger me dead, Tel, don't you ever give up? You'd drive any man to drink! Talking of which…" He gave me a wink, turned off the tranny and walked out of the yard, leaving me with a tapestry of thoughts to unravel.

The Cross Key 7

ALTHOUGH DAD AND I would go down to
Melbourne on a regular basis, it was always to the
fruit and veggie markets. It turned out that each time we
went down to Melbourne, we passed pretty close to Tom's
hotel, the Cross Keys, a big barn of a place in Pascoe Vale.
Above the pub itself were the rooms where travelling reps
stayed overnight. Dad had told me about these places and
had intimated that there were 'other things' that happened
in those upstairs rooms which weren't for the ears of an
innocent country boy like me.

"There's a lot of shagging and gambling goes on in those
upstairs rooms," Kev informed me as we parked his truck
around the back of the hotel. "Don't agree with it myself,"
he said with a poker face before opening the door and
slamming it after him.

It had taken a great deal of my persuasive power, plus Kev's suggestion that it'd do me good, to get away from Yarramah for a few days. When he added that it'd help broaden my mind, Mum suggested that in his company it wasn't my mind she was worried about! But eventually she acquiesced.

"You take good care of my boy, Mr O'Ryan," she said as I climbed into the cab, "otherwise I take care of you."

Dad intervened by putting his arm around her and giving her a hug. I checked the rear-view mirror as we drove away and saw her pull a handkerchief from her pocket and dab tears from her eyes. That choked me up a bit as Mum never cries.

"Good woman, your mum," Kev pronounced, and we drove on in silence.

Tom was older than Kev. If Kev could be described as a rough diamond, Tom was definitely a polished one, yet they both admired each other greatly. Neither were big on emotions.

"G'day, Tom."

"G'day, Kev. Beer?"

"My bloody oath. A midi of VB for me and a lemonade for the young fella. This is Tel, he's my offsider at the works when he gets time off from his old man's shop and studying. He's a good toiler when he stops leaning on a shovel."

"Good to meet you, Tel. First time in Pascoe Vale?"

"Yes, Mr O'Ryan."

"You can call me Tom as long as you're okay with me calling you Tel." Turning to his brother he asked "Where are you staying, Kev? Need a room here?"

"I'd appreciate that. And one for the young bloke, but not near any of those good-looking sheilas. Can't be leading him into temptation, his mum'd have my guts for garters!" They both laughed at my discomfort.

"It's a big place, Tom," I offered, gazing around the huge bar with its long counter and several sets of beer taps. Glasses were lined up in sparkling perfection on shelves behind the bar. A sign at the end said 'Gents'.

Following my line of sight, Tom informed me that no ladies came into the bar.

"There's a small room out the back where a few of our senior sisters meet to have a beer and a good old yak, but it'd take a mighty confident young lady to come into the front bar at swill time."

"Too busy having fun upstairs," Kev observed before changing the subject. "Any news for Tel?"

"Sort of. There's a lady who works at Births, Marriages and Deaths who gets me to place her bets on the gee-gees. If her old man ever found out he'd divorce her. He's very straight laced and a pillar of the church. Can't stand the man myself, but that's life. Anyway, Mavis said she'd make some inquiries on my behalf. I'll probably be seeing her tonight as there's a big race carnival up at Moonee Ponds this weekend which should bring the punters out in droves."

"Any of your horses in the race?"

Tom's face was a picture of conspiracy. "Not one of mine Kev, but I can tell you who's going to win if you'd like to have a small wager."

"You know me' Tom. Don't bet, don't swear, don't drink, don't shag and don't tell porky pies!" The two of them erupted in laughter, so I joined in.

The grand staircase which led to the upper level of the hotel was almost as wide as our shopfront. The wallpaper had seen better times and the old chandelier was missing a few bulbs, but to a kid from the bush it was all hugely impressive.

"Keep your mouth closed, Tel. Makes you look like you're a few tiles short of a roof."

"Be nice to the lad," Tom chided his brother gently.

The corridor was almost as wide as the staircase.

"It's big enough to play a game of footy," I joked.

"Believe me," Tom sighed, "we've had a good few try over the years!"

Despite the massive grandeur, it was all a little bit faded, even to my rose-tinted vision. The cream-coloured doors sported coffee-coloured stains and a mosaic of chipped paint. Around the handles were grubby scratch marks and greasy palm prints. Some of the door numbers seemed to have nodded off and were dozing peacefully, slantedly suspended from a single screw. The faded carpet exuded the beery smell of the downstairs bar reflecting, no doubt, the many glasses of VB spilled upon it.

I was given a room at the far end of the corridor, which seemed to make Tom and Kev happy.

"Should be fairly quiet down this end. It's well away from the bar area," was Tom's explanation. He unlocked the door using one of those old-fashioned keys with long metal shanks. It had a lump of wood attached to one end with the name Grace burned into it. "It's the name of a friend of the first owner," Tom explained.

"Good looker too, if I remember correctly," Kev added. Nothing was said between the two of them but the air was thick with innuendo.

The room sported a single bed, which was just as well as nothing else could have fitted in. There was a sash window at one end, which rose up to the height of the distant ceiling. It was embraced by sun-bleached, threadbare red curtains, which in their youth were no doubt intended to block out the streetlight placed strategically outside of it. The peeling ceiling held a single bulb light suspended from a short cable about twelve feet above the ground. Still, it was all I needed. I'd brought a rucksack for my change of clothes, into which Mum had managed to squeeze enough food to last a mini ice age. By the time I'd unpacked, I silently thanked her for her efforts as I was starving. Having satisfied my hunger, I opened the window to let in some fresh air along with the sound of the Melbourne traffic. Then, on an impulse, I decided to explore the neighbourhood.

Locking the door behind me, I headed down to find Tom and hand in the key, not because I'd lose it, but because it was too bloody big to put in my pocket.

"Just heading out , Tom. That OK with you?"

"No worries, Tel. Melbourne is at your disposal, just don't believe half the things you see or hear. Need some funds?" He began to dig into his pocket.

"No thanks, Tom, I'm fine" I began to say, but he interrupted.

"Come on, son. I don't often get a chance to share some good times with friends of Kev. Just think of it as family, eh?"

"I really appreciate that, Mr O'Ryan," I murmured.

"It's Tom, OK?" he reassured me, before patting me on the back and nudging me through the frosted glass front door and out onto the street. "Best be back before the bar opens or after it's closed," he called after me, "otherwise it's total chaos here!" He gave me a happy wave, turned and was swallowed up by the maw of the hotel.

City life is not just busier, noisier and dirtier than country life, it's also a lot more fun! It must have taken me a good half hour just to walk a couple of hundred years down the street. The shops were amazing. There was so much colour and such variety that I almost got a headache soaking it all in.

I called into a coffee bar where a jukebox was playing. The tables were filled with young people sitting around and drinking milkshakes or sucking up the latest craze – iced coffee. I ordered a choc milk and sat down in the corner, trying to be invisible. There were posters on the wall of Elvis and of a guy who was called Johnny Hallyday, whom I'd never heard of.

"He's French," a friendly female voice said. She was sitting behind me in a booth with four other mates, one of whom appeared to be Italian, with his jet black hair thrown back in a Brylcreemed quiff. I didn't think he was enjoying his milkshake as his face would turn cream sour!

"Is he a pop star?"

"I think so," she replied, "the owner's wife is French so she gets all the latest fads from France. It's really good actually because I'm studying French at school. I'm Mary, by the way." She offer her hand over the back of the booth. I took it and felt the soft coolness of her grip. She spoke in a refined voice, not at all like the way Goggs or Yabby yakked on.

"Tel's my name. It's short for Telemachus. It's Greek," I added as if she hadn't worked it out already.

"Is that wog annoying you, Mares?" the slicked-up Italian called out from his side of the round table.

"Everything's fine, Gino. Just talking that's all."

I exchanged meaningful stares with my Italian friend, none of which were of the friendly variety.

"Who's he?"

"That's Gino and he's a bit protective of me. He seems to think that we're dating, but we're not really. Where are you from, Tel? You're not from around here, are you, otherwise I'd have noticed you before." A slight colour rose in her cheeks.

"I'm from a small town up on the Murray. I've come down with a mate to do some research into my family tree. We're staying at his brother's place, at the Cross Keys Hotel, apparently he's got a contact at the Births, Marriages and Deaths place."

"That sounds interesting."

"Yeah," I continued, trying to sound as matter-of-fact as I could. "Our family tree is a little complicated what with some of us being Greek and others from England and Ireland."

"I think our family must be really dull and boring. As far as I know, everyone from way back when were born and raised in Victoria. How parochial is that?"

I refrained from showing my ignorance and asking what parochial meant, but simply said, "You don't look boring to me in the slightest."

Gino must have had great hearing because he chose that moment to stand up, which was a bit unfortunate really as he knocked his milkshake into his lap, aggravating his already foul humour. "You back off, chummy. She's my girl and I don't like her talking to no wogs."

"She seems to have a great way with words, actually, Gino. I'm surprised you can understand what's she's saying." There were definitely times when I should keep my mouth shut, but there was this little imp inside of me that just couldn't stop itself. "Still, I suppose that cold milk has shrivelled the size of your brain." The giggle that erupted around the table was like petrol to a fire.

By the time the owner of the milk bar had lifted the counter and headed towards us, Gino was attempting to escape from his seat and grab me by anything that he could reach.

"Outside, the two of you. I'm not having any bad behaviour in my place. OUT. NOW." We left like the two disgraced youth that we were.

Gino turned to me. We were about the same build, the same age and the same height, but then I was Greek and he was Italian, which was why he threatened me with all sorts of recriminations in his own colourful language.

"My, my, Gino," I answered sarcastically, "did you swallow a dictionary or something?"

I sauntered off along the street, protected by the broad daylight and the thronged pavement. I made it as far as the racecourse and stood in the shadow of the stands watching the horses go through their paces. They were gorgeous specimens of horse flesh with a sheen to their coats, which only highlighted their meticulous care.

"G'day, Tel."

Only one man could say my name like that.

"G'day, Kev. What are you doing down here?"

"A schoolmate of mine works in the bar. Good bloke. He's the only honest person I know who doesn't drink beer."

I wrestled with what he'd just said, and then gave up deciding that it was another of Kev's classic red herrings.

"Enjoying yourself?"

"Yeah. It's been good. Met a nice girl in the local milk bar called Mary. She's probably a little bit too posh for me, plus the fact that she was with a real loser of an Italian called Gino. He got us chucked out of the place for misbehaving." I looked at Kev to see if he'd be upset. He just arched his eyebrows, swivelled his nose to one side and gave a loud sniff.

"Are you heading back now? If you are then I'll come with you. I need to pop into the betting shop. Tom's good for a solid tip, but then, I'm not too bad either." With that mysterious insight we headed back up the street to Pascoe Vale.

When we got to the TAB, Kev told me to go on ahead and he'd catch me up. I sauntered along in front of different shops on the opposite side of the street to which I'd travelled down, but found myself feeling slightly stale from everything on offer, because in reality there was nothing that I needed.

"Hey, wog."

I knew that voice. Turning around I found not only my Brylcreemed buddy, but a whole bunch of them.

"You've got a big family, Gino," I said with bravura, at the same time feeling somewhat unsettled inside.

"You've got some nerve, bushman. You come down here and think that you can just do as you want? This is our town, wog."

"It's true then what they say about the wops," I replied, stamping my feet on the pavement. "They came, they saw and they concreted!"

That probably wasn't a wise thing to say so I took off down a side street. It didn't take long before they'd cornered me outside of a derelict shop. Geez, I was out of condition. They formed an intimidating semicircle in front of me, with Gino standing in front.

"You asked for this, wog."

"You got a problem *dickhead*?" It was one of those John Wayne moments, except in this case it was Kev standing on a parked car looking down on the guys in front of me. "You hard of hearing or something?" he asked. "I said, have you got a problem?"

"Piss off, old man," Gino shouted, "this is none of your business."

"Too bloody right it's my business. If you want to pick on someone your own size, there's plenty of midgets down at the circus, you clown." Kev had a way of delivering a line that diminished his opponents in their own eyes. "Well, dickhead, I'm ready." With this he jumped down from the car and walked towards the group. It was like the parting of the Red Sea. "The trouble with Melbourne, Tel, is that there's a lot of rubbish on the street and sometimes you step in it. C'mon. Let's go." With that we walked through the gang and left.

I must admit that I was a little shaken by the whole thing. Being alone, surrounded by a mob of blokes who were prepared to kick the S-H-one-T out of me was not a nice place to be. "Thanks, mate," was all I could immediately muster. A little further down the street I asked him, "What if they'd not backed down?"

"Not my problem, Tel. They're just a bunch of kids playing games. The thing is, when they're faced with their own weakness they find it hard to cope. Then it's easier for them to back down. Mind you, if they went the biff they'd have made a bad mistake." People talk about men of steel like Superman and stuff like that, but that's all comic book stuff. With Kev, when he needed to, he used words of steel and was prepared to back them up with action; but most times he didn't have to.

"You ever been in a fight, Kev?" As I looked at him I added, "Silly question, eh? But did you ever lose?"

The eyebrows arched for a moment, the nose twisted and the sniff came. "There was one bloke back in Yarramah, big bastard. I shoulda kept quiet because there was no way I could fix him up." The eyebrows went up in resignation. "He gave me a good working over. I was sore for days afterwards. Good bloke though. Met him some months later and we had a few beers together. He's living somewhere up in Queensland now."

The words of that conversation may have drifted off into the noise of Pascoe Vale but they lodged in my mind for a long time afterwards. Fighting never settles an issue, it just delays the solution, which is sitting down and having a good old yak together.

I left him at the door to the bar and headed for the main entrance. On arrival at the desk, I was informed that I had a guest waiting for me in my room. That muddled my mind. As I headed up that baronial staircase I hoped and prayed that it wasn't Gino with a few of his mates. Needless to say, I was pleasantly surprised to discover Mary standing at the window, watching the world go by beneath her. She turned as I entered the room.

"I'm so glad that you're OK," she said in genuine concern. "Gino can be very…" she searched for an appropriate expression, "*Italian* on occasion. He seems to think that I'm his girl – which I'm not."

"No need to explain. Nothing happened. We did bump into each other but he came to his senses. He's probably a very nice guy," I proffered, trying not to sound too patronising. "There's always been a bit of history between the Eyeties and us Greeks. It's just jealousy, really, as we Greeks taught them everything they know."

"I suppose it's the same with the French, seeing as how you Greeks founded Marseilles as well."

Now I was swimming well out of my depth. This girl had obviously had a very thorough education in classical history. "Yeah, well, there aren't too many French in Victoria so it's never really been a problem. You did know that Melbourne…"

"Has the second highest population of Greeks outside of Athens? Yes, I did," she interrupted, with not the slightest sign of smugness on her pretty face.

"So what are you like with footy teams?" I challenged her. We both held a serious face for about five seconds before succumbing to giggling like the kids we were. Yes, I did fancy her because she was drop dead gorgeous, but even better than that she was a really decent human being.

We sat on the bed and yakked away for the next hour. I knew it was an hour because a roar steadily grew inside and out of the building. Knowing that the chaos wouldn't settle until at least six o'clock, we just ignored the noise and chatted away to each other.

I was telling her about Kev when there was a knock at my door and a voice called, "Are you there, Tel?" The man was telepathic!

"Cometh the hour, cometh the man," I whispered to Mary and opened the door. With Kev, you could never tell whether he'd had one beer or ten, he always looked the same. But if he'd had ten, and if there was a sheila about, then a lecherous look would definitely surface on his face.

On this occasion he'd obviously only had three or four. In one quick glance he'd checked Mary out and decided that she was OK.

"Tom's asked if you want to come over to his place for tea. You can bring your friend with you if you want."

"Thank you very much, Mr O'Ryan," Mary began.

"The name's Kevin O'Ryan, but you can call me Kev." He held out his hand for her to shake.

"Pleased to meet you, Kev," Mary continued, "and thank you for your invitation but I really must be getting home, I have so much homework to do and Mum will be wondering where I am." Turning to me, she smiled, saying, "It was really great to meet you, Tel, perhaps we could catch up tomorrow?"

"Yeah, that'd be great, but I don't know where you live."

Mary reached into her bag, pulled out a sheet of paper and wrote down the address. Instead of giving it to me, she gave it to Kev. "Mr O'Ryan probably knows the area better than you do, Tel. Bye." And with that she was gone.

"Come on, Casanova," was all he said. I grabbed a jacket and headed off down the corridor after him.

"Where does she live, Kev?" I asked, struggling to get my arm inside the sleeve.

"On the wrong side of the track."

"You mean the railway line?" I asked, sounding dumber than I really looked.

"Essendon is where all the Prods live. If you're a Mick or a wog you've got diddly squat of a chance of getting a guernsey with her or her family."

"You're pulling my leg … aren't you?"

"Nope."

"They're that parochial down here?"

"Worse." The man used words like a sniper uses bullets.

"But I can see her again, can't I?" Even to my own hearing, I sounded like a little boy who'd just been denied an ice-cream.

"Never make a decision on an empty stomach. I'm starving."

For a bloke who hadn't lived in Pascoe Vale for years, I was amazed at the number of people who shouted out 'G'day, Kev', or 'G'day, Rooster'.

"Played a bit of footy in my time. Could have been top flight but I was too lazy to train. Still, I captained the local team for a couple of years." The eyebrows arched briefly at the memories. "Good fun."

Tom's house was a large suburban, brick and tile, double-storied place on a quarter acre block.

"Mortgaged to the eyeballs," Kev said, pushing through the gate. "Does too much dough on the gee-gees. G'day, Tom," he said to his brother, who was sitting on the verandah enjoying the early evening breezes. "It was pretty busy down at the Keys today. The barmen were like bricklayers with six arms."

"Good evening, gentlemen," Tom replied. He had a large glass of red wine in his hand and it probably wasn't his first. "Beautiful day. Richard's inside. Do you want him to get you a beer?"

"VB for me. What'll you have, Tel?"

"Same for me, please."

"Get smartypants a lemonade or something," was Kev's smooth response.

We spent the evening at Tom's place, with the two brothers sharing stories of their shared past. Of how their dad, a good and decent man, used to ride his bike around the area selling insurance. They swapped stories on their sisters' most recent relationships, but being brothers, they were almost certainly wrong. Although there were plenty of stories and family 'in' jokes, you could tell that they were both fiercely protective of them.

During the course of the evening, Tom slipped half a bottle of beer into my lemonade. "Just between you and me, eh? Wouldn't own a hotel if I didn't promote my own product, would I?" We clinked glasses and drank to life.

I think that it was their kindness more than the half glass of beer which made me feel more relaxed. They may have been as odd as two left feet, but in my mind, the O'Ryan family were pretty special.

On our way back to the hotel, I couldn't restrain myself from asking Kev, "So where does Mary live?"

"That's the trouble with you Greeks, all you think about is girls. Don't worry, I'll draw you a map tomorrow. It's about a ten minute walk but mind your p's and q's if you don't want to start a riot."

I went to bed that night thinking about everything that had happened. City life was certainly more exciting, louder and seemingly full of unexpected dangers than I'd expected. I loved it!

It can't have been long after I'd fallen asleep when I was woken by the rhythmic sounds of busy bed springs coming from the room next door. It was accompanied but the guttural growl of what, at first, I thought to be a dog out in the corridor. Then the penny dropped. Hoping that it would soon all be over, I turned on my other side and waited … and waited … and waited.

Eventually, I couldn't take it anymore. I went out into the corridor and pounded on the next door bedroom. "Fair go mate, some of us want to sleep around here." Perhaps I was a little hasty and hadn't thought through the consequences of my actions, but in an instant the door flew open. A huge man lifted his ham-sized fist, and launched it straight at my head.

The truth will out

IN THAT SUSPENDED second I listened for the sound of an owl, or some indication that I would wake up in the courtyard of Odysseus' villa. But life, or maybe the gods, often surprise by doing the unexpected.

"Oi, Donk. What's going on?" It was Kev! He had a piece of paper in his hand, which I later learned was the map to Mary's house.

The calloused knuckles were barely an inch from my face. "This dickhead was disturbing my rhythm, Kev. I was just going to suggest he went bye-byes until I'd finished my business with a certain young lady."

"Hello, my darlin'. How're you going, Kev? Long time no see." To call the owner of that voice a 'young lady' would be stretching one's imagination to the limits. Not only that, but I was surprised that the *knowing look* she sent Kev didn't knock him over, it was so thick with suggestiveness.

"G'day, Suzie. You're looking alright for a sheila with poor eyesight!" He ambled along the carpet until he reached the three of us. The scent of Suzie's perfume was enough to stun an ox. Or maybe an ass! "Shame you're wasting time with a young fella like Donk here. A girl like you needs a real man."

"You took the ... words ... right out of my mouth, darl." A jet of cigarette smoke left her red, rouged lips as she looked at Kev through smudged mascaraed eyes.

"Aw, come on, Kev. Give a bloke a fair go! I may be young but I'm real keen."

"You can say that again," Suzie said in a stage whisper. The three of them began to laugh like old friends.

"Tel, meet Donk and Suzie, two of Pascoe Vale's best students. God knows at what though! Tel's down with me from Yarramah for a few days. First time he's stayed in a posh hotel like the Keys. But you know what Greeks and shagging are like, always keen to impress the ladies." I must have blushed to the roots of my hair.

"Any time you have a spare moment love, I'd be happy to give you a few tips." My new friend blew smoke at me accompanied by a friendly smile.

"Here's the thing you wanted, Tel," Kev said, handing me the paper. "I suggest you stick some cotton wool in your ears when you go back to bed, Donk takes his work very seriously."

"Thanks, Kev," I mumbled to him. "Sorry," I mumbled to Donk and Suzie.

"No hard feelings, son," said Donk, engulfing my hand in his huge mitt. "Good to see yer, Kev."

"I meant what I said," whispered Suzie as the door closed behind her. I shuddered to think whether she was talking to me or to Kev.

"See you, Tel," said Kev, and he was gone.

Surprisingly, I slept like a log for the rest of the night and woke totally refreshed. I had a few dollars in my pocket so I searched out a small cafe for breakfast. With map in hand it wasn't long before I was crossing the railway line and heading into Essendon.

Reading maps proved to not be one of my strongest points – they don't cover it much in high school. Or maybe it was that Kev wasn't much good at drawing them. But after screwing up courage and asking a kindly shopkeeper where the street I was looking for was, I eventually found myself outside of a semi-detached 1930s home with a manicured front garden. Everything about the place was regimented down to the last 'T'. The hedge was trimmed to within an inch of its life; the hosepipe coiled tightly on its hook by the tap; the edges around the flower beds as crisp as a paper cut; and there was not one dead flower to be seen – all had been removed, allowing only the living to show their wares.

Mary was in an upstairs room. I guess she must have been studying at her desk by the window as she had a pencil in her mouth. I saw her smile and wave then disappear. I was aware that my heart was starting to race, but, taking a deep breath, I walked up the pristine pathway and knocked on the front door. The knocker had barely finished its job before the door was whisked open to reveal a lean man with cropped hair and piercing blue eyes. He smiled at me with one of those veneered smiles that you know conceals a troubling alter ego.

"Hi," I began, "I'm Tel. Is Mary home?"

"It's OK, Dad, Tel's a friend of mine. He's down from the country and I asked him over." Her father never took those mild blue eyes off me. Without a word he pushed past me and went off around the side of the house. "Don't mind about Dad, he won't bite you." She sounded light-hearted, but I wasn't convinced.

"Nice place you have here, Mary. Our front door is a fruit and vegetable shop but it works on the same principal!" She showed me into the front room, which connected with the kitchen from whence came the sounds of the local radio station. Being Melbourne, the commentary was about footy and the racing results.

I scanned the room; like the front garden, it was immaculate. Even the regulation family photos were lined up with military precision along the sideboard, along with a display case holding three medals awarded to a Sergeant Hoplite. "Are they your dad's?"

"Yes. He's a bit of a hero around here. He got those in Vietnam, although he doesn't talk about it. One's for bravery and the other two are the usual ones soldiers get for going into a war zone." There was a melancholic tone to her voice but I kept quiet. I'd already heard a bit about the vets who'd come back from Vietnam, none of it good either.

"How is he?"

Mary looked at the medals, avoiding making eye contact with me. "He's not the same man who left here three years ago. But hey," she went on, determined to be happy, "at least he came home. So many of them didn't or couldn't. Come into the kitchen and meet Mum."

Back at home in Yarramah, entering the kitchen was like the Catholic idea of transubstantiation: where food is turned into life. Dad often referred to Mum as a real miracle worker; even Fr Bob called her the blessed one!

Mary's Mum was the total opposite of a Greek mum. Small, neat and wearing a pinafore that was perfectly pressed, she had the whole place spotless and every jar on display labelled and filled to three-quarters full.

"I'm thinking of making some tea cakes, Mary, do you think Dad'll like them?" There was some doubt in her voice and I immediately sussed that Mary was the only one who might have any influence over her father. If I was correct, then the gods of war had played havoc with his mind and he had to be handled with consummate care. From my brief meetings with Mary, I was confident that I was on the right track.

"I think that'd be a great idea. Dad loves tea cakes, especially the ones you make with the sultanas in them. By the way, Mum, this is Tel. Tel, this is my mum, Mrs Hoplite."

I held out my hand but she didn't see me. She'd gone ashen white.

"I haven't got any sultanas, Mary," and she began to panic.

"Don't worry, Mum, I'll go and get some. Tel, are you coming?"

"He can stay here and help me in the garden." The air went frigid as glances shot between the three of us. Mr Hoplite had appeared and just stood there watching me like a spider.

"Sure thing, sir," I said, sounding as bright as I could. "Careful crossing the road, Mary," was my weak attempt at humour. It failed miserably.

"I'll be back in ten minutes." With that she was gone.

He stood there watching me with those blue eyes. I was beginning to think the man was totally unhinged.

"Follow me."

We went out into the garden, leaving Mary's Mum to rebuild her confidence and then attempt to construct the most perfect of tea cakes.

"We need to dig up the veggie patch. Tomatoes are finished, lettuce were useless and the radishes are beginning to bolt. So pull everything out, pile it over there and then start digging."

"Yes, sir."

Being under military rule is different from working in Kev's cement factory, even though the latter is much harder. I set to with a vengeance and soon had the compost heap piled high with dead plants. Dark patches had appeared in the armpits of my best blue shirt. "Mind if I take my shirt of Mr H? Mum'll kill me if I rip it or something."

"You got a vest on?"

"Yessir." I was beginning to feel like a bloody soldier.

"Permission granted, then." Bloody hell, he was treating me like one of his squaddies! I started to wonder how far away the shops were that Mary had gone to. I stepped back and stumbled into an old rosemary bush and the scent of it immediately filled the air.

"Be careful you..." Those steely blue eyes had turned grey in their narrowed aperture. But rosemary reminded me of Athene, and I thought to myself that if she could help someone like Odysseus for over twenty years, then she might spare ten minutes for a Greek boy doing it tough with a damaged Hoplite!

"I hear Nam was a tough place, Mr Hoplite," I began, having determined to talk and talk until Mary returned to save me. "A couple of my mates' dads were killed over there and my best mate, Goggs, well his old man came home, but he sort of didn't either." I grabbed the shovel and began turning the brown soil over.

"It's real tough for him because he loves his old man and his old man loves him, but somehow they've lost the ability to talk to each other. They kind of dance around the subject but never jump in and see what happens. Kev, he's the bloke I work for in the summer holidays, well, Kev says that the vets saw stuff that no man should see and they don't want to load that sort of stuff onto their kids. So they just keep to themselves or catch up with their old mates and sit and stare into their beer.

"Kev reckons they're lost and don't know their way home. The strange thing is that the kids themselves feel just as lost in their own homes too. Kev reckons, and it's real strange coming from Kev as he never hugged a bloke in his life, but he reckons that if the vets could just hug their kids and let their emotions out then things would be a whole lot better. Naturally, it won't change the past, but it might change the future."

I was aware of a silence as I paused to gather my breath. I realised that I'd already dug up half the veggie patch. I turned to see how Mr H had taken my stream of consciousness. Tears were rolling down his face. Mary was frozen in the frame of the back door.

"Shit," I mumbled to myself. "I've put my bloody foot in it again."

Mary was the first to move. She came over to her dad and ever so gently put her arm around his now shuddering shoulders.

I went out through the side gate, leaving the metallic click of the latch as the sole reminder of my presence. I was amazed to see a brand new Ford Fairlane parked out front with Kev sitting in the driver's seat.

"It's Tom's. Get in."

"What are you doing here?"

"'Thanks for picking me up Kev'," was his sarcastic response. "Tom knows the girl's dad. Vietnam vet. Being doing it tough, apparently." His eyebrows arched briefly. "Some of those blokes can get a bit toey so I thought I'd call round just to make sure."

"So why are so many of those vets just totally screwed up?" For the first time, Kev gave me a really dark look.

"That's the trouble with history, everybody forgets it until it happens all over again. What happened in Vietnam? Blokes who shouldn't have guns were given bloody great big ones and told to go and shoot them at little yellow men living in another country. And guess what? The little yellow men were much smarter than the smartypants in America and Australia thought. They got themselves some bigger guns and fired them back at the Yanks and the Aussies.

"So what happened? Thousands of the poor conscripted bastards who were sent over there get killed, and ten times that number of the people living in villages in Vietnam – kids and women as well mind you – they get blown away too!

"And let's not forget the rest of the disaster. If you weren't one of the poor bastards that got shot, then you probably came home with a dose of the clap or hooked on drugs – those Yanks love their purple hearts, and I'm not talking about the medals, either."

Kev rarely stayed angry for long. If there was no-one to take him on in a fight, then his challenges tended to dissipate into a well-reasoned insight.

"Don't know what it's like for the little yellow men in Vietnam, but the blokes who came back couldn't cope with what they'd seen and done. Couldn't dump it on their families, so most of them just bottled it up. Some used guns to kill themselves – most of them are still struggling. Tom told me that Mary's dad tried to top himself once but one of his mates talked him out of it. His family don't know that, though. Mary seems a good kid so keep that under your hat. Maybe a nice Greek boy from Yarramah might bring a bit of sunshine into their lives, eh?"

"More like heavy rain, I'm afraid. I tried to impress them with my great insight and left them all in tears!"

Kev leaned forward and turned the ignition key. The six litre motor throbbed into throaty life.

"Good car. Tom keeps it in top order." He clicked on the radio and soon the runners in the next horserace at Ballarat were being announced. "Funny thing about life, it never turns out as you'd expect."

I was invited to go to the races but opted instead to stay in my room and read. Too much had already happened in the last twenty-four hours and I still hadn't got any further with the reason we'd come down in the first place. I must have dozed off for a while because when I woke up, the light in the room suggested that it was late afternoon. I splashed some water on my face from the small hand basin in the corner of the room.

A knock at the door made me jump. Rubbing my face dry, I reached across and opened the door. I didn't know who I expected to see, but Mrs H was the furthest from my thoughts.

"May I come in, please?"

I opened the door wide and quickly secured the only chair from under the small desk and offered it to her. With a benign smile she accepted, which left me to sit on the bed like a recalcitrant child waiting to be told off by a disappointed parent.

"Your visit caused quite a stir, Tel," she began. "I doubt our family has ever experienced anything like it since my husband left for his first tour of Vietnam."

"He went more than once?"

"Unfortunately, yes." Her eyes dropped for a millisecond before she looked directly at me again. I was beginning to get the impression that there was more to this mousy lady than met the eye.

"Alan didn't think he'd even get called up. He was born on the 29th of February, which as you know is a leap year, and he didn't think the army would be clever enough to work that one out. Unfortunately, they did, and he was one of the first to get his papers.

"Like most of them, he was part excited and part terrified and we played along with it all, telling him he'd be a real hero and that he'd come home with so many stories to tell our children. We'd only had Mary at that time and we'd been trying for some years for another … but that's another story. We were all so full of trust and self-belief back then.

"Alan would write to us, but everything was censored. But at least as long as he wrote, we knew he was alive. More and more people were getting telegrams telling them terrible news. Every wife and mother lived through terror while their men were away. He did his first tour and seemed so happy to be home. He was back at work within a few weeks and life seemed to get back to normal. He'd catch up with his vet mates and often come home worse for wear, but we didn't mind too much.

"One night he came home and told me that he'd signed up for another tour. I was so shocked that I couldn't speak. All I could say was 'if that's what you want darling', and then he was gone. He'd told me that he had to go back because his mates were still over there and they needed him. It's only recently that I've come to understand the deep bond those men developed."

Mrs Hoplite paused, almost overcome with visceral emotion, but she recovered, gaining my deepening respect.

"After you'd left today, Alan told us about what happened on that second tour…"

"If you don't want to talk about it, you don't have to, Mrs Hoplite." I blustered trying to save her from the obvious distress of it all.

"I'm fine, thank you Tel. I think I need to talk to someone about it just to get it clearer in my mind and for some reason, you're the only one I could think of talking to who wouldn't offer advice or patronise me.

"His unit was out near a village called Son My. The Americans had been having a tough time of it with Communist insurgents infiltrating the villages and burying land mines and booby traps around the area. There were lots of casualties on both sides. Alan said that a lot of the soldiers were using drugs to keep awake and drinking lots of beer and spirits to go to sleep. It wasn't a happy place. Alan got to know some of the people from Son My and they responded to his kindness by bringing him and his friends fresh fruit and home-cooked meals. He says that the Vietnamese are very happy people.

"One night, all hell broke loose. The Americans had decided to eradicate the enemy force in Son My and My Lai, which was the adjacent village. Captain Calley led the offensive, which he called a liberation but which turned into a massacre. What happened there broke Alan's heart, and his spirit, too. He and some American troops tried to defend some of the villagers, but it was Armageddon. Men, women, children and infants were murdered: women were gang raped and their bodies mutilated. Alan says that the real death toll was over five hundred innocent souls. The men who tried to shield the villagers were shunned by their own soldiers and called traitors when they returned home."

I was totally drained by what I'd just heard. It was – is – the most terrible thing I'd heard of in all of my short life. Yet sitting in front of me, on a rickety wooden chair, was a small mouse of a woman who, it turned out, had the heart of a lion.

"I know all of this must be very distressing for you and I didn't come here to upset you, but I thought you'd like to know that what you said to my Alan had a deep effect on him. He hadn't told me any of these things until this afternoon. He'd have come himself if he could ... but it's better that he's home with Mary. I don't know what sort of miracle caused all of this to happen or what will happen in the future, but I wanted you to know that whenever you come down to Melbourne, our home is your home."

Standing, she held out her hand. "I'd best be off now. I have to get the tea on the table. The world may have just turned on its head, but tea still has to be prepared."

We shook hands like strangers. I've forgotten what I mumbled to her. My brain hadn't caught up with all the information it'd just received. I stood in front of the sink with its peeling, silvered mirror and stared at my reflection.

"Wow, wow, bloody WOW." It wasn't not Shakespeare, but that was all I could come up with. I shook my head and left the room as if trying to escape the terror that had just been relived within its walls. I skipped down the stairs two at a time. The roar from the bar indicated that swill time was in full swing.

"Tel, over here son." It was Tom. He'd been talking to a middle-aged woman who looked like an overripe thirty-something. "Hazel, this is Tel. He's the lad I was telling you about."

The woman sized me up and down and came to the conclusion that she liked me. Not that she was my sort AT ALL, but under the circumstances I had to be polite.

"Nice to meet you, Hazel."

"The pleasure's mine, Tel," she said with a twinkle in her eye.

"Tel's trying to get hold of his birth certificate, Haze. He doesn't have much to go on apart from the fact that he'd been left in an orphanage somewhere in town. If Tel can discover who his father is..." He left the end of the story dangling enticingly in Hazel's imagination.

"Give us the details and I'll get back to you tomorrow."

"You're not going in to work tonight just for me, are you?"

"Sorry, sonny, you're a gorgeous hunk of Greek goodness, but no, since that bloody war started we've had a baby boom and everyone is working overtime to keep up. And it's double time working on a Saturday night so I'm not complaining. Perhaps another time, eh?"

"I'll write down my details for you," and hastened over to the reception to get some paper. Mission accomplished, I returned. "I can't thank you enough, Hazel."

"You don't have to son. We've all got some missing links in our families. With Tom's mob, it's his brother Kev," and she roared out laughing.

"Are you having fun at my expense, Haze?" Cometh the hour, cometh the man …

"My bloody oath I am, Kev. You owe me big time."

"I always pay my debts, Haze, you know that," and he gave her one of his more knowing grins. He gave a loud sniff, sculled the last of his beer and said almost in passing, "Might have to get Tom to post the news to me in Yarramah, Tel, we've got an early start in the morning. Gotta stop off and see a bloke about a dog on the way back."

Tom and Hazel took this piece of information in their stride as if it was the third item on the local news.

"But, Kev," I began.

"You got a problem with that, Tel?" he asked. It was a simple question but there was just a hint of menace in his voice. "You've won the lottery already with the parents you've got. It's hardly likely that you're going to win big again, is it? Hazel here will get you the information you want, and does it really matter if you get it tomorrow or later next week?"

The kid in me was screaming, 'Yes it bloody well does', but a new and expanding part of my mind shouted back, 'Hold on kiddo, Kev's right – you still need to think through the consequences of all this stuff.'

Taking a leaf out of Kev's playbook, I turned to Hazel first and said, "If I was ten years older, Haze…" and gave her an outrageous wink. "But seeing as I'm not, I just want to thank you from the bottom of my heart for what you're doing. I really appreciate it."

"Aww, Tel," she responded, enveloping me in her ample bosom and stunning me with her chemical aura. "I don't reckon you need to wait ten years," and planted a lipsticked kiss on my forehead. Turning to Tom and Kev she added, "I could never resist a Greek bearing gifts."

"I never knew you had a classical education, Haze." This was Tom, who was looking genuinely surprised.

"Them nuns at Sacred Heart might have been a bit keen on the strap, but they gave you a bloody good education, too." Leaving her calling card imprinted on both their cheeks, she pulled on her gloves, saying, "Well, I must be off. Someone's got to do the work around here. I'll drop the stuff off to you Tom, once I get it, and you can send it on to Kev – OK?" With that she was gone.

"Good sport, Haze." This was Tom again.

"Not your sort eh, Tom?" Kev turned to me adding, "Tom likes skinny birds. Big sheilas just don't do it for him do they, Tom?"

"Mind your own business," he said and left us to oversee closing time.

"Talk to you later, Tel. I've still got a couple of beers to finish. I'll call you at six in the morning. Be ready."

Athene and Yolungoo

I REALLY WANTED TO see Mary before I left Melbourne, but at the same time, I didn't want to intrude after Mrs Hoplite's visit. I wasn't much cop at writing and I knew that once I'd got home, there was no way that Mum would let me use the phone to ring long distance to Melbourne, so my only option was to call around to see her.

I headed off back to Essendon and rehearsed what I would say in the twenty minutes it took me to get there. In my imagination I had her sitting at her desk gazing out the upstairs window again, sucking on her pencil.

But she wasn't. There wasn't a sign of life at the house. Later on I was to discover that her dad had taken them all to the local RSL club for supper for the first time since he'd got back from Nam.

To say that I was deeply disappointed would be an understatement. Standing there, trying to work out what to do next, I was disturbed by the deep rumble of what sounded like laughter coming from the other side of the street. Half expecting to see an escaped maniac, I peered around anxiously. To my relief, standing under a tall ghost gum tree was the rotund figure of a professional-looking man who was staring up into its branches.

"Beautiful," he said out loud to me, without taking his eyes off whatever it was that had attracted his attention.

I wandered over in his direction and gazed up into the branches. As I scoured the branches, I became aware that the man was humming a tune in a very pleasing tenor tone. The street lamps had just come on and were casting an orange glow into the darkening canopy.

"What are you looking at?" I asked, but before he could reply the distinctive call of an owl softly filled the air. Then I saw the bird itself. It was a beautiful barn owl, contentedly looking around and occasionally twisting its head down to stare at us.

There's something hypnotic about watching owls. Perhaps it's those large black, blinking eyes, or maybe it's the incredible way they spin their heads almost there hundred and sixty degrees without it actually falling off.

For a few glorious moments, a deep bond existed between the owl, a portly professional man and a lovelorn

Greek kid. We humans stood there watching for God knows how long in blissful silence: a silent communion of souls.

Then, with a whiffling sound from its wings, the owl took flight and disappeared into the darkness.

"Amazing."

"He comes here most nights around this time of year. Beautiful bird." Looking around at me the man asked, "You're not from around here, are you?"

"No, sir," I replied. "My name's Tel, it's Greek, and I'm from Yarramah up on the Murray. I'm a friend of Mary's." I nodded in the direction of her house.

"Mary's a nice girl. Yarramah, did you say? You don't happen to know Kevin O'Ryan, do you?" he chuckled to himself. His whole frame rocked with happiness. "One of the biggest larrikins you'll meet in a month of Sundays. If you see him, send him my regards." Holding out his hand he introduced himself. "Barry Forrester. I used to work up in your part of the world. One of my favourite memories was going camping down at the bends with my sons. How long are you in Melbourne for?"

I was on the cusp of saying that Kev was driving me back when a loud motor bike went by and the pillion passenger shouted something obscene at us.

"A certain lack of original thinking, eh? One of the draw-backs of living in the city is the lack of bush humour," he commented dryly. "So, are you here for long?"

"No, sir, I leave early tomorrow to head back up. I was hoping to catch Mary before I left, but it looks like they've all gone out."

"I'll tell her you called. Where in Yarramah do you live?"

"My dad has the fruit and veggie shop on Lisle Street."

"I know it well. You must be Peter's son." He reappraised me through his glasses, which he proceeded to take off and polish with a clean white handkerchief. Without his spectacles his face looked almost innocent, or perhaps it was just the recollections of happy memories from the distant past which amplified his kindness.

"The last time I saw you Tel, you were this high," he said, holding his hand at the level of his knee. "Do send your parents my best regards. It's a small world, eh?"

"Thank you, Mr Forrester. Nice to meet you," and we shook hands.

"Amazing creatures, owls. Did you know that they have something to do with Greek gods?"

We both briefly stared back into the now blackened umbra of the tree. "I'd heard that."

"Well, I'd best be off. Good night, Tel." Barry Forrester disappeared along the pavement, the brightening street lights giving him an almost other-worldly look. I'd only known him for such a brief while, but had decided that he was a good man.

Kev banged on my door smack on six o'clock, but I was already up, which pleased him. "First Greek I know who could get out of bed before midday, apart from your old man, but he's almost an Aussie anyway."

After giving the room a final check over to make sure I hadn't forgotten anything, we headed on down to the hotel lobby to say our goodbyes to Tom, which amounted to a 'See ya' from Kev and a handshake from me.

"Kev's not big on emotion," he said in an aside.

"I'd noticed that, but he makes up for it in other areas, Tom."

"I know. Best brother I ever had."

Kev was Tom's only brother! It seemed like both the O'Ryans were smart alecs!

We climbed in the truck and made off for the Hume Highway and the road home. "I want to stop at Benalla, but that's about two hours away. The truck radio's stuffed, and you can't hear the tranny with the window open so you may as well grab some shut-eye if you want to."

I created a nest for my head with my rucksack and slowly drifted off to the sound of the Ford at three-quarters throttle.

I was woken by the jolts of the truck as it entered a rutted, dirt track that obviously hadn't received much attention for quite some time. I'd also dribbled on my chest!

"You take your medications today?"

"You sound like my mum," I replied, wiping my shirt dry. "Anyway, I don't see why I should keep on taking them seeing as I haven't had any fits for ages. I reckon that doc in Wang got it wrong."

I paused, remembering what Athene had said. "And anyway, we Greeks heal really well. What do you reckon, Kev?"

"Do as you're told and take the bloody tablets, that way you won't keep pestering me!" He turned the truck around in front of an old weatherboard cottage causing a cloud of dust to fill the air. As it cleared it became pretty obvious that the place needed a bit of care and attention, especially the rusty roofed lean-to which acted as a front verandah.

"This is Phil's place," he said, as the hinges of the Fords door squealed to announce his exit.

Sitting on an old, abused sofa was a dusty older man who had a kelpie dog sleeping next to him, its head resting on his lap. The man, a half-smoked cigarette between his lips, idly stroked the dog's head while propping a stubby of beer on the other leg with his free hand.

"You know smoking stunts your growth, don't you?"

"Geez, you're a grumpy bastard, Kev. Wanna beer?"

"It's the only reason I stopped."

"Help yourself mate, they're in the fridge. Does the young fella want one?"

"My oath he does, but he's not having one. I'm not game enough to take on his old lady. Got any cordial?"

"What's that? There's water in the tap though."

Kev pulled the reluctant flywire door open and went inside.

"G'day, Phil, I'm Tel."

"G'day, young fella, good to meet you. Welcome to my country."

Seeing my slightly confused look, he was about to say something, when Kev reappeared after knocking the cap off his beer bottle. He wiped his lips and informed me with arched eyebrows, "Phil's a boong, Tel. Not that you can tell 'cos mostly he's mostly a white fella. It's a bit like you're a wog but you're an Aussie, too. Me? I'm Aussie through and through, that's until you get to mi' Irish ancestors who were sent out here as convicts. Phil here's a gun shearer. Been at it for years. If he hadn't spent all his wages on grog and backing the wrong horses, he could probably buy the whole place back for his mob."

"And if you didn't spend half your time drinking beer and shagging sheilas, Kev..."

"Then you might as well shoot me," he interjected , and the two of them roared with laughter together.

"He's a good bloke, is Phil," Kev informed me earnestly. "Best worker I ever came across. Where did your mob come from, Phil?" he asked as he drained his stubby and headed back to the fridge to replace it. "Want another, Phil?"

"Thanks mate. Know any Abs, Tel?" he said, turning his shy gaze on me.

"No," I answered, feeling a tad flustered. At the front of my mind was the fact that it had only been in the past couple of years that the Aboriginal people had been given the right to vote and been accepted as equal citizens. Up until this very moment I'd managed to avoid prodding that hornet's nest of social history, and now here I was talking to one. It was a curious fact that even though I'd lived in Yarramah all my life, I'd never met an Aboriginal before. "No, Phil, you're the first one."

"No need to be scared, son, we don't eat whities anymore," and his face broadened into a soft smile. "Thanks, Kev," he said taking the proffered beer from his hand and taking a small sip.

"My mob are the Yorta Yorta people. We come from up near Barmah Lake, up near Deniliquin. You know the place, don't you, Kev?"

"Yep. More flies than mozzies but both of them will drive you mad. Denny's not a bad place. Although it's too hot in summer for my liking."

"Our people have lived in the area for two thousand five hundred generations. Work that out if you can. We were here when the land up near Denny tilted thirty paces and caused the lake to form, and the one at Moira. Beautiful country."

"Have you got any family, Phil?" I asked in all innocence.

"Family," he laughed, "well, probably about one or two hundred, I suppose."

"How do you work that out?" Even Kev seemed incredulous.

"Well, I grew up near the lake with Mum, Dad and mi' sisters. Dad went off shearing and never came back, then Mum died when I was about seven and Grandma and Grandpa took me in with some other cousins. We had loads of aunts and uncles who used to keep us in line, as well as the other family members who weren't in our blood line but who were still our family, if you get me.

"My gran gave me my totem, the black cockatoo, and so anyone who has the same totem is considered family. You white fellas never really bothered to learn about our traditions so you don't understand all this. But to us, it's a spiritual thing. It binds us to each other and to the land."

"That's the trouble with boongs," Kev teased, "ask 'em to tell you a story, and they will!" He took a pull on his beer. He often hid his wisdom behind his warped humour.

"Must have been tough to have been a boong back then. Mind you, it hasn't bloody changed much, has it?" Kev arched those eyebrows of his and gave a trademark sniff. "Maybe if those do-gooders had known all that stuff before they came up with the crazy idea to take your kids away from you and put them in mission school, just because their old man had done a runner or got on the turps and ended up in the clink, your mob might not be so pissed off with us whities."

For some reason I began to feel guilty about what Kev was talking about, as if somehow I'd been complicit in what had happened to those kids who'd been taken from their Mums and Dads.

"There was some terrible stuff that went on in them schools, but the old mission fathers knew how to give more than just the strap." His dog must have been dreaming because he gave a whimper, lifted his head for a second just to check everything was OK and then went back to sleep.

"Old Fr Murphy reckoned that the Greeks had it all worked out pretty sweetly until Socrates arrived. Up until then there'd been a bit of balance between working, living, paying respects to the spirits, poetry, plays and stuff like that. Then along comes Socrates, Plato and their mates with their scientific stuff, making up all those lists and questioning everything. Fr Murphy, well he reckoned that somehow, with all their thinking and analyzing, somewhere along the line they lost their souls. An' for a white fella, I reckon old Fr Murphy got it just about right."

I was mesmerised. I'd never heard anything like it before, and this coming from a black fella. I glanced at Kev.

"I haven't got a clue about what you're talking about, Phil, but I reckon we white fellas gave you black fellas one good thing."

The sound of two beer bottle necks being clinked together symbolised their mateship, just as it has done with so many blokes over so many decades here in Australia.

"See, I told you," Kev pronounced. "He's a bloody good bloke!"

"I don't know who my real dad is."

I was amazed that I was the only one who was surprised by what I'd just said. The other two took it in their stride.

"Depends how you define a dad. In our culture, family and connection to the land is real important."

"My old man was a decent sort." Kev sniffed as his nose turned characteristically to the left indicating that he was about to say something important. "It's a big ask, bringing up kids."

I felt let down.

"I reckon there must be a bit of Ab in your parents, Tel. I can't think of another mob who would have done as good a job on you, even if they were your real parents."

"It's about connection, Tel. Once you've made that connection with what's real important to you, then you'll find your spiritual home."

"Crikey, Phil, you're getting worse than Fr Bob raving on at Sunday Mass."

"You haven't been to Mass for years, you pagan bastard," came the quick-fire rejoinder and the conversation moved on to talk of sheep, fencing and cockies who might be interested in buying some of Kev's new concrete fence posts.

After a few names had been gathered and a few more beers drunk we got back in the truck and headed back to Yarramah. Kev was in great spirits and talked non-stop all the way from Benalla until he dropped me off outside the front of the shop in Lisle Street.

"Thanks, Kev. That was great."

"I'll let you know as soon as I get anything from Tom. Say g'day to your Mum and Dad for me," and with that he roared off up the street in the direction of his home away from home at the hotel.

Even though it was Sunday, Dad had the shop open. It was the only place open, apart from all the churches in town.

"How was the big city? Kev didn't lead you astray, did he?"

"He better not have!" That was Mum, who was washing down the floor around the cold room we had out back.

"No, it was great. I met his brother Tom. He's a nice man. And I met a girl called Mary whose dad was in Vietnam. He'd had a hard time there." My voice trailed off and glances flashed between Mum and Dad.

"Are you OK?" That was Dad. He might have been the hardest worker in town, but he had a heart as big as Kev's truck.

"Nah. All good. I met a man called Mr Forrester, as well: he said he knew you and to say hello."

"Mr Forrester, he a good man. Helped us with getting Australian citizenship." The way my mum said 'Os-traaa-lian' always made me smile. "How his beautiful wife? She a very good woman for an Italian. And her so small with those five crazy boys. How she do it I never know!" She attacked the floor with greater vigour as if trying to shoo the five Forrester boys out of her shop.

"I only met Mr Forrester."

"You remembered to take your tablets, son?" The conversation was halted by the arrival of a customer.

"I'll go and shower. See you later."

"Lunch will be ready in an hour."

Mad as a Chook

W HEN I GOT home, I decided to keep taking my meds just to please Mum and Dad, though I truly believed that I wasn't an epileptic anymore. Despite them slowing me down, I determined that now that summer was here, I would get back into sport at school. Thus it was that I spent most evenings down at the oval practicing my 'leggies' in the cricket nets with a couple of mates.

I know there are a lot of people who don't get cricket, and I can understand their point of view: when a game that you play stops for tea breaks AND lunch, and then, even after five days, can still end in a draw may seem a little anachronistic to people with shorter attention spans!

But playing the game is different. It has a cadence to it that is almost restful. Out there, guarding the boundary of a cricket pitch, your imagination can roam through some vast open spaces. I suppose it's a bit like how the boundary guards in Troy must have felt when the Greeks laid siege to them for all those years. Usually not much happened, so you had time to think of home, family and life in general.

Life after school wasn't just about practising bowling, but it did help free my mind so that I could study better when I got home. I may not have been the sharpest knife in the drawer, as Kev would say, but I was up there in the top three or four in all my subjects and in history I was *numero uno*!

In that final term at school, Dad let me off my chores after school as he knew that the pressure was building towards the big exams at the end of the year. He got Kath to come in and help, though the dear lady spent most of the time perching her bulky frame on a stool and trying to stay cool. Dad didn't mind too much about that because it had the advantage of her being able to keep her eagle eye on the till. Even though everyone knew everyone else in Yarramah, from time to time a blow-in would arrive who'd try and put one over on Dad. One thing about Kath, she may have had the softest heart in north east Victoria, but her vision was still twenty-twenty and she never missed a trick!

Mum and Dad told me that they didn't worry about me going down to the oval, even though it meant extra work for them, because they knew that it was good for me to let off steam. In hindsight, I have to admit that at the time I never stopped to think how much they put themselves out for me.

When it was stinking hot, I took my school books with me so that after a session in the nets, I'd jump in the river to cool down. Then I'd study at one of the local picnic benches until the mozzies came out for their evening meal – me!

One Saturday, when it was even too hot for the flies to come out, I was doing some study down near the river at a place where the occasional breeze brought some cooling relief, when I heard a car drive past on the track that led into the state forest. Usually, only the local rangers were allowed to use the track, but at night courting couples were known to use it for a clandestine kiss and a cuddle. So I didn't take too much notice when I heard the engine, only looking up briefly from my books before returning to my studies.

I was deep into the early European settlement of Tasmania and was not particularly enjoying what I read. The slamming of the car door made me look up again. I could just make out the outline of a battered old Holden parked in the bushes about fifty yards away. I recognised the car but couldn't place who owned it.

I was on the verge of packing up and going home when I heard someone sob loudly. What made me freeze was that it was a bloke who was sobbing his heart out. I stared across at the bushes where the car was and made out the figure of a man standing at the front of the vehicle with a rifle butt stuck against the front bumper, the other end in his mouth.

"Oi, stop mate. You can't do that! STOP!!" I got up and began to sprint in his direction, yelling for him to stop.

I only made five paces when the gun went off and the back of his head exploded in a spray of blood, brains and bone.

The shock of it all stunned me. The sound waves of the gunshot reverberated through the air, causing birds to flee their perches, screeching madly. My brain screeched, too, because I suddenly remembered whose car it was.

It was Chook Harris'.

There was no way I was going to go any closer, so I took off back down the track and headed straight to the police station, which was only a couple of hundred yards away. Needless to say, on a Saturday afternoon it was shut, but Sergeant Little, who lived next door, was happily mowing his front lawn, so I managed to flag him down and frantically tell him my news.

"Calm down, son. Are you OK? Now just calm down and tell me exactly what happened."

I took a couple of deep breaths and recounted my story in a steadier voice. I told him that I thought it was Chook who had topped himself. "Why would he do that, Sergeant?" I pleaded with the good man, as another wave of horror hit me.

"Chook's had a pretty tough life and he hasn't helped his own cause by drinking himself half to death. It's the worst combination in the world, guns and alcohol. But you leave it with me. You go home to your parents and I'll take care of everything. I'm afraid that I'll have to get you come down to the station after the weekend to make a statement though, but that's just a formality really. I'll have to inform the Coroner, too, because there'll have to be an inquest."

That was too much information for me to take in but what did stick was "go home". So I did.

Kath was perched on her stool by the till and immediately knew something was wrong. I could see her nudge Dad who had his back to me. "You OK son?" he asked, concern filling his voice. "Not another fit?"

"It's Chook, Dad. He just shot himself. He just blew his own head off," and I dissolved into great heaving sobs.

He embraced me with his strong arms and stroked the back of my head, making soothing sounds as he did so. Gently he turned and led me inside, to where Mum was making the evening meal. Once I'd settled, bookended between those two loving souls, I told them everything that I'd seen and heard. Kath leaned against the door post and looked on with deep concern.

"Why would he do that, Dad? I know he was a drunk, but to shoot yourself through the mouth..." The horror of it almost made me want to vomit.

"Chook didn't do himself any favours, Tel." It was Kath who spoke. Her voice was rasping a little. Kath was known to have shed tears if she saw a cat with a dead mouse, but this time she sounded different. "I'm just so sorry you had to be there when it happened." She reached into her bag and took out her ciggies along with her little ashtray. Kath was a tidy person at heart. She lit a cigarette and took a deep pull on it.

"Chook liked to make out that his old man had beaten him when he was a kid and that his mum had abandoned them. It was all bulldust. His mum was a lovely lady. She didn't abandon them. Chook made it all up. His dad may have been a drover, and yes, he had to go away a lot, but he never left them short of anything. They lived out near Barham just the other side of Cohuna.

"I'm sorry to say that the bloke wasn't right in the head. When he landed in Yarramah he told all sorts of porky pies, and to start with, most people believe him. Mind you, he wasn't a bad looker back then," she added with a slightly wistful tone to her voice, "but he was always a terrible drunk and a wicked liar."

"No-one should ever do what he did to himself," I pleaded.

"Darl," Kath continued, reverting to her more usual loving mode, "he's at peace now. Let him explain how he lived his life to the good Lord. I've no doubt he'll be forgiven, but I'm sad to say that there's a ton of people here in town who won't be sad to see the back of him."

Just then the ambulance went down the street with the siren howling.

"That'll be Jim off to pick up the body." Silence filled the room.

We heard a car stop out the front and a door slam shut.

"I'll go," said Kath, stubbing out the remains of her cigarette in her ashtray and snapping the lid shut. In a couple of moments she returned with the sergeant.

"Just checking to see how the lad is."

"That's kind of you, Ted," my father said.

"No problems, Pete. It's a pretty awful thing for a young lad to see. I've seen a few in my time and it still turns my stomach. I've got the doc in my car so I'd best be off. Call into the station when you can, Tel, and I'll take your statement. See ya," and he was gone.

"That silly stupid Chook, why he scare my poor baby like that? If I knew he go and do that, I break his neck!"

Trust Mum to bring us back into the moment. She stared back at us as we began to smile.

"What's so funny?"

Odysseus bends
his bow

I DECIDED TO GO to Chook Harris' funeral. Fr
Bob had agreed to do it, although no-one was certain
whether he was a Catholic or not. Kath reckoned that his
parents had been Micks but Chook had no papers in his
house to either confirm or deny it.

He had lived in a small shack on the outskirts of town
where he appeared to have lived most of his life on an
old couch on the verandah. It was a bit like Phil's place
in Benalla, but while you'd describe Phil's house as basic,
Chook's place was a pigsty. The guys from Vinnies cleaned
it out and took everything straight to the tip. There was
nothing salvageable in the place apart from a couple of
old faded photos of what we think were his parents. But

knowing Chook, he might just have picked them up on the street.

Fr Bob did a great job at the service. There were only a few of us there. Kev turned up, as did the owner of the hotel.

"Only right," he said, "seeing as he paid the mortgage for the past ten years!"

Dad came with me but Mum didn't. I thought she might still be mad with him but Dad told me that she was making some food for everyone for after the burial. Typical of Mum really: always thinking about feeding her men!

It was the first time that I'd been to the cemetery. It was a dry, desolate place but you couldn't avoid the headstones with all their loving words. Each one of them told the story of a soul in one sentence. One stayed with me. It was a baby's obsidian headstone with golden lettering: "In loving memory of … aged 33 days, now in God's care." That made the tears flow for me.

We gathered around the freshly dug grave where Fr Bob stood like a tower of strength. He said the words over the coffin, blessed it with holy water and then in a flash it was swallowed up by that deep, unseeing world below. Slowly we all shuffled away, leaving Kath alone to stand by the grave. We watched from a distance as she opened her handbag and poured the contents of a half bottle of whiskey over the last mortal remains of Chook Harris.

"He tried it on with Kath way back, when he was just a plain scallywag. That was before the drink got to him and he became an all-out drunk." Kev had appeared at my shoulder. "She gave him the bum's rush but he kept pestering her. I had to have a word with him to tell him to back off. I don't reckon Kath ever forgave what he tried to do to her. That's until now."

Back at the hotel, a small wake was held for him. Mum had done us all proud with the food she provided and soon an air of merriment replaced the shadow of death that had so recently permeated all our thoughts.

"Have you heard anything from Tom?" I asked Kev.

"Nope."

Changing the subject, as that conversation seemed to have hit a concrete wall, I followed up with, "Will you need a hand up at the yard this summer? School's finished until the exams and the final results won't be out until the New Year."

"Maybe." The eyebrows had arched which indicated that he was moving into a good mood.

"There's no-one else in town who can lean on a shovel like me, Kev. You said so yourself."

"OK young fella, you're on. Take a few days off after your exams and then call down to the yard and we'll see if you're up to snuff or not." With that, he gave me a wink, lifted his glass to his lips and took a long drought. Placing his glass back on the beer mat he added, "And don't worry about Tom. As soon as he gets word from Haze, he'll send it on to me. Now bugger off. You're too young to be in the bar ... isn't he?" he said to the owner who was just happened to be passing by.

The weeks passed and life became consumed by studying, eating and sleeping, broken only occasionally by meeting my mates at Barrett Park and kicking the footy around. Mum and Dad's routine never changed. Their life revolved around the shop and sorting out the bad apples from the good ones.

A tinge of guilt never left me during those waiting times. Why did I really need to know who my real parents were? How could anyone have better parents than me? I'd sort of determined that whoever turned out to be my real parents, then I'd still not move from Yarramah and I'd still call Mum and Dad, Mum and Dad. But even in that, I felt as if I was deceiving myself as well. I'd started the ball rolling and now there was no escaping the outcome, whatever that turned out to be.

There was a glint of happiness during those study times. One Sunday, Kev appeared at the shop looking very dapper. Even Dad was impressed, although Mum remained suspicious. "Won the lottery, Kev?" That was Dad.

"Sort of," came the odd reply.

"Of course he has," said the pretty pixie of a woman we knew well from the pharmacy, and who was now slipping her arm behind Kev's elbow. Mum's eyebrows shot up in disbelief.

"Cheryl Mary? You know Kevin O'Ryan?" Disbelief hardly covers the tone of her voice: shock would be closer, but would lack the obvious respect that she held Cheryl Mary in.

"G'day, Mrs Alysandratos. Beautiful day, isn't it?"

Dad stepped in to speak because Mum seemed to be struggling with her words.

"I'm glad to see that Kev's come to his senses at last, Chez. But keep him on a short leash," he said as he took a bite out of the apple he was shining.

"Aw, Kev's just a big puppy dog, Pete," she replied, and a glorious smile accompanied her light and lilting voice. Kev seemed a little peeved.

"Chez!" The word was a curious mix of command and endearment.

"Come on, Kev. Let these good people get on with their work. Good luck with the exams Tel, we need people with brains around here." She rolled her eyes in such a playful manner as she tugged Kev off in the direction of her home in Moat Street.

"You've gone very quiet, Nana." This was Dad's attempt at quiet humour.

"That Kevin O'Ryan is a very lucky man. Cheryl Mary, she a good girl. He'd better take good care of her or else." Dad and I eyed each other off across the shop.

"I'd better go and do some more study. See you," and I made a quick exit to the house, leaving the two of them to dissect what they'd just seen with their own eyes.

Even though I was a good student and expected to do well, I'd really no idea what I'd do when I finished school.

Mum and Dad were keen for me to go to university and that meant either Sydney or Melbourne. Melbourne was full of Greeks, and Mum had some cousins there, though strangely she never went to visit them. Dad had some rellies up in Sydney but what with keeping the shop open seven days a week and the distance, he hadn't been up to see them for years, and vice versa. So all in all, neither city held too much attraction for me. I'd been pretty happy with life in Yarramah, but as I grew older the place seemed to get smaller and smaller.

Still, life was pretty sweet. Good home, good food, camping down at the bends, footy, cricket and the girls who seemed to like a certain Greek Adonis called Telemachus Alysandratos, so I was in no big hurry to move on. But the challenge was there and it was looming up before me faster and faster.

"Go for one of the professions, Tel." That was Kev as I was brushing up around the yard. My brain was brimming with facts and figures and pushing a brush around Kev's place seemed to help cement them in the right spot, if you forgive the pun. Well, it's not really a pun, but you get the point.

"Don't think I could be a priest, Kev, don't they have to remain celibate?"

"Celibate means they can't get married. Nothing about not shagging as far as I know."

"Really?" I exclaimed. "I never knew that. Still, I'd like to have kids one day."

"Once you've had a few kids you might want to change your idea about becoming a priest, but I get what you say."

I began to follow his line of thinking. "The law could be a go-er but it seems so dry and dusty."

Kev skimmed the top of the post he'd just finished filling the mould with. "Remember the bloke you met in Essendon, the one near Mary's place?"

"How did you know about that?"

"You talk in your sleep dopey! Well, at least that's what you did in the truck on the way back up from town that time." Nobody had ever told me that I talked in my sleep, but then again, who was going to tell me? "Barry Forrester, he's a solicitor and he seems to be doing alright. There's talk of him owning a vineyard down near Mornington, so I reckon he's learned how to cope with settling all that dust and dryness of the law!"

"Does he really?"

Kev's eyebrows suggested that I'd just said something really stupid.

"And then there's Doc Buckley. Have you seen his house? I reckon he makes a decent quid, and he loves his golf. Not bad either."

"Do you play golf?"

"Yep. Mind you, I never thought it fair to hit a ball when it wasn't moving." The grin on his mug informed me that he'd just told a joke.

"Is there anything you can't do?"

Kev paused to take a slug from his bottle of water. "I could never go out with a big bird. Can't stand 'em if they're carrying too much condition. Kath's OK, but that's because she's Kath. I like thin ones." This pronouncement was made with sober thought and not the slightest indication of any lascivious intention.

"Thanks for that, Kev" I replied ignoring his last comments. "That's really helpful!"

Young love
strikes – again

JULIE WAS IN the same year as me but we didn't see much of each other as we were studying different subjects. I'd been studying history, geography, general science and English literature, and she'd been the only girl in the maths, physics and biology classes.

"Are you going for medicine?" I asked her when I'd bumped into her at the supermarket a few weeks before the final exams.

"That's the plan, although it's such an impossibly high score. No-one from Yarramah has got into medicine for years, as far as I know." She looked a little dejected as she spoke.

"Well, there's always a first time for everything," I suggested. "Kev reckons the world'll be a much better place when there are more female docs."

"Mr O'Ryan said that?" Disbelief permeated her voice.

"Yeah, well, I thought it a bit strange as well, but somehow that guy always seems to be ahead of the game." I paused for effect. "And he suggested that I take you to the drive-in with me on Friday, it's Steve McQueen in *The Thomas Crown Affair*. I hear it's really great."

"I didn't know you had a car," she said, her voice now blending both incredulity and optimism.

"Actually, I don't. But Dad could drive us out there. We can chuck a couple of deck chairs in the back, pack the Esky with whatever we want to and we'd have the best seats in the house."

"What happens if it rains?"

"Aw, c'mon Julie! Where's your sense of optimism? If you're game, then I reckon you'll be able to study like a Trojan afterwards and smash the final few weeks of study, then it's medicine here I come!"

"Tel, you're such a dag," she laughingly replied. "But I'll check it with my parents first and if it's OK with them then it's OK with me, too."

Walking the short distance back down to our shop didn't leave me with much time to work out how to get Dad onside. I knew he'd come up trumps, but like most things in life, there's always two sides to a bargain. It turned out that my side of the agreement was to really knuckle down and give those last few weeks of study a real shot. Nearly everyone who was sitting the final year exams was suffering from terminal study fatigue, but now I had a real reason to finish what I'd started. To my mind there weren't many better reasons to keep my promise than to do it for Mum and Dad: a night out at the drive-in with Julie just happened to be the cherry on the icing on the cake.

On the night of the movie, Dad dropped us off at the drive-in. The warmth of the unusually hot springtime day had lingered on into the evening. Not a single cloud blighted the pale blue western sky. As the evening slowly drew on, stars began to pop up like celestial mushrooms. Soon the Southern Cross was visible, along with Orion's Belt and the Pleiades.

As the blues darkened to black, a sudden orange light glowed near the horizon. "What's that?" asked Julie in mild alarm.

"Burn off," I replied with a calm, albeit slightly cocky authority. "Normally the farmers burn off their stubble at the end of harvest, but apparently someone must have missed out and so now they're trying to catch up before seeding time. Beautiful, isn't it?"

We both sat there, along with all the rest of the patrons in their various vehicles and watched the glow slowly fade from the horizon. Then the screen flashed an image of a lion roaring and we knew the film was about to begin.

It was a great movie. "I've always loved Steve McQueen," I whispered to Julie, "especially that scene in *The Great Escape* where he tries to jump over the wire fence on his motorbike."

"Me too, though you can keep the motorbike."

I looked sideways at her. She continued to stare at the screen before bursting out giggling and squeezing my hand as she did so. That simple gesture caused havoc in the circuitry of my brain cells.

"He's really good-looking," I said, trying to cover my reaction. "I think his mother must have been Greek." After a short pause it was my turn to squeeze Julie's hand and smile into her pretty face as the popular theme tune heralded the start of the main film.

It was a great night. Mum had done us proud with the food and the weather was perfect for a night at the drive-in. When the final credits began to roll and the sounds of various engines began to start up, we packed our gear up and decided to walk back into town. It was only a couple of kilometres away from home and the half-moon gave enough light for us to easily see what was on the gravel at the side of the road. Several people offered us a lift, and one or two wise guys offered us some unwanted advice.

We met Dad coming out to collect us about half-way in. "Thanks Dad, but we're fine ... really."

"Why don't you dump your stuff in the back then, and I'll meet you back at home? You're sure you don't want a lift home Julie? I know he comes from a good family, but you know what they say about Greeks."

"Thanks, Mr Alysandratos, but I think I can handle the situation. Your son is quite the gentleman. And do thank your wife for the wonderful food, it was really delicious."

"Will do. See you soon. Bye," and his red tail-lights disappeared up the road before he did a quick U-turn and headed back to town. He waved happily as he went by.

"Your dad's so nice."

My mind flashed to the face of Hazel and the impending arrival of the information she had dug up on my real parents. Suddenly all the colour was sucked out of my evening, causing me to fall quiet.

"You've gone quiet. Anything wrong?" Julie asked, genuinely puzzled.

"Nah. I think I ate too much. It's just a bit of stomach-ache. I'll be fine soon."

As we passed the first house on the edge of the town, I inadvertently rubbed against a bush, releasing the scent of rosemary into the warm air.

"Did you know that the goddess Athene is associated with the scent of rosemary and owls?"

"Owls?"

"You know, those feathered creatures with big eyes that sit in trees at night hooting at us humans."

"I know what owls are," Julie said, giving me a push in the back. "But I bet you don't know why owls never get married though."

"Huh?" was my spontaneous intellectual response although I was beginning to enjoy life once more.

"Owls never get married because they haven't got the wit-to-woo."

"That's terrible," I groaned and tickled her. Julie set off up the street giggling and I gave chase. Julie was a pretty good runner! We made it as far as Moat Street before the two of us staggered to a walk to regain our breath. I took her hand and we walked slowly along until we came to Lisle Street. Dad's car was parked outside of the shop and I could see his figure hunched in the driver's seat.

"He's waiting to see if you need a lift home."

"Aw, he's so nice."

Every young couple has experienced that hiatus in time when you're unsure as to what to do next. Should we give a gentle peck on the cheek, should it just be a reassuring squeeze of the hand or a full-blown hug?

Julie made the decision. With a quick peck on my cheek she took my hand and crossed the empty street to Dad's car.

"Thank you so much, Mr A. It really is so kind of you."

"No problem at all, young lady. Tel here has told us lots about you."

"Dad," I winced as my cheeks reddened in the low light.

"I hear you're thinking of studying medicine. Well good on you, young lady. The world needs bright, smart and kind people to look after them, and from what my son tells me, that seems to sum you up. Hop in." He leaned across and opened the passenger door. "Are you coming, too, Tel?"

"I think I can trust you to take Julie home safely. Some of us need to study some more before we go to bed. Thanks for a wonderful evening Julie." Her dark eyes smiled back at me, then they drove off.

The gods intervene

EXAMS LOOMED AT the rate of an express train and in the twinkle of an eye they were over and done with. I couldn't believe that I'd finished school, or that there'd be no more exams or that my life was about to change forever.

"If you go to university, Tel, you'll still have plenty of exams to take." Kath was sitting on the stool by the till lighting up a cigarette while perching her ashtray on her ample thigh. "I reckon you should go to Melbourne. It's only three hours away and your dad is always up and down from there. Much easier than Sydney. If you want to study some more you could always do a postgraduate degree in Sydney, but if I were you, I'd go to Melbourne." The idea of Kath being an expert on university life amused me.

"When I was in the air force, I met a lot of officers who'd been uni students, in fact, some of them still were. The nice ones went to Melbourne though. Lovely lads they were too."

She took a deep pull on her cigarette and sent a narrow stream of smoke out into the air of Lisle Street. "It's a good university, Tel. Good place for either the law or medicine."

Sometimes Kath seemed pretty simple and, truth be told, missing a few tiles from her roof. But behind that simplicity was a sharp and active mind. It was just that she didn't need to use it that much in Yarramah, and she much preferred the slow, quiet life that it provided her with. Her husband had died young and she was childless. I think that's why she was so kind to everyone. She saw everyone as a part of the family that she was never able to have.

"Thanks, Kath." I went over to her and gave her a hug. She crooned her thanks.

"Now look what you've made me do," she said, smiling happily as she dabbed the tears away from her eyes.

"I'm going camping down at the bends this weekend so I'll think about it. At the end of the day it all depends on what score I get."

"You'll breeze through, Tel. You're like your dad, and like that bloke you're both always going on about, is it Ulysses?"

"Odysseus, Kath. The Italians call him Ulysses but Odysseus was a Greek. Have you read the *Iliad*?"

"I don't need to, what with you and Peter always talking about it."

"That reminds me," I mumbled. There was a section at the end of the book that I wanted to re-read, so I decided to take it with me when I went camping. "Thanks, Kath. See ya!"

Mum and Dad thought it would be good for me to spend a night out at the bends. "You make sure you take your tablets, and no drinking beer like that Kevin O'Ryan. And make sure you eat the food I pack for you." No need to explain who that was!

"Dad, I've been thinking of going to uni in Melbourne, depending on the score I get."

"Sounds like a reasonable idea, son. You're pretty smart and it'd be a waste of your talent sticking around Yarramah for the rest of your life."

"You've done pretty well for yourself, Dad."

"Back then there weren't that many options, Tel. And as you know, it's hard work keeping this business going seven days a week almost three hundred and sixty-five days of the year. No time for getting sick and apart from that long weekend we grabbed recently, your mum and I haven't had a break together for..." He looked across at Mum for inspiration.

"What we need a holiday for, eh? Life always a holiday whenever I am with my boys." We ate in silence, her words permeating my conscience.

That night I took out Homer and flicked through to near the end, to the bit that had been niggling me and began to read:

He spake; a son of Dolius at his word
Went forth, and, coming to the threshold, stopped.
He saw them all at hand and instantly
Odysseus bespake thus with winged words:
"They are upon us, we must arm at once."
He spake, they rose and quickly were in arms.
Four were Odysseus and his friends, six
The sons of Dolius. Old Laertes then,
And Dolius, put on armour with the rest,
Grey-headed as they were, for now their aid
was needed. When they had all clad themselves
In shining brass they threw the portals wide
And sallied forth, Odysseus at their head.
Now Athene, daughter of Almighty Zeus,
Drew near them. She had taken Mentor's form
And Mentor's voice. Their much enduring chief,
Odysseus, saw her and rejoiced and said
To his beloved son Telemachus:—
"Now wilt thou, of thyself, Telemachus,
Bethink thee, when thou minglest in the fray
That tries man's valour, not to cast disgrace
Upon thy forefathers—a race renowned
For manly daring over all the earth."
And thus discreet did Telemachus reply:
"Nay, if thou wilt my father, thou shalt see
That by no lack of valour shall I cast,
As thou has said, dishonour on thy race."

Laertes heard them and rejoiced and said:
"Oh what a day for me, ye blessed gods,
Is this! With what delight I see my son,
And grandson rivals on the battlefield."
And then the blue-eyed Athene, drawing near
Laertes said, "Son of Arcesias, loved
By me beyond all others of my friends,
Pray to Zeus' blue eyed daughter and to Zeus
And brandish thy spear and send it forth."
So Athene spoke and breathed into his frame
Strength irresistible. The aged chief
Prayed to the daughter of almighty Zeus,
And brandished his spear and sent it forth.
It smote Eupeithes on the helmet's cheek.
The brass stayed not the spear, the blade passed through,
And heavily Eupeithes fell to earth,
His armour crashing round him as he fell.
Then rushed Odysseus and his valiant son
Forward, the foremost of the band, and smote
Their foes with swords and lances double-edged,
And would have struck them down to rise no more
If Athene, daughter of the god who bears
The aegis, had not with a mighty voice
Commanded all the combatants to cease:—
"Stay, men of Ithaca; withhold your hands
From deadly combat. Part, and shed no blood."
So Athene spoke, and they grew pale with awe,

And fear-struck; as they heard her words they dropped
Their weapons all upon the earth. They fled
Townward as if for life, while terribly
The much-enduring chief Odysseus raised
His voice and shouted after them, and sprang
Upon them as an eagle darts through air.
Then Zeus' son sent down a bolt of fire;
It fell before his blue eyed daughter's feet,
And thus the goddess to Odysseus called:
"Son of Laertes, nobly born and wise,
Odysseus, hold thy hand; restrain the rage
Of deadly combat lest the god who wields
The thunder, Zeus' son be wroth with thee."
She spake, and gladly he obeyed. And then
Athene, the child of aegis-bearing Zeus
Plighted, in Mentor's form, with Mentor's voice,
A covenant of peace between the foes.

When you read a book several times you always discover something new.

I hadn't realised that old Laertes had thrown the final spear. I'd forgotten that Odysseus had asked Telemachus not to disgrace the family and I'd forgotten that it takes a god to sort things out!

Families! Such a strange grouping of people, and yet they've been the glue of civilisations for aeons. Only our egos stand in the way of making them work.

Now here I was, with the best parents in the world, and I'd begun something that would definitely bring disruption, dishonour and perhaps despair on all of us, and God knows how I was going to dig myself out of the hole I'd dug for myself. In a fit of pique, I threw the book across my bedroom in disgust at what I had unleashed.

"You OK, Tel?"

"Fine, Dad. I just dropped something."

"Good night, son. See you in the morning."

"Night, Dad."

The next day I was up bright and early. I'd picked a Thursday to go camping because it would be easier to get a quiet spot. On the weekends, families tended to go out along the river to camp, which was great, but the place could get pretty crowded and noisy. Mind you, on some weekends, the local cockies' kids tried out their trail bikes on the tracks along by the river, and they made a hell of a noise, and usually a hell of a mess, too.

And don't get me started on pig shooters. It's not that I like feral pigs, they're ugly bastards digging up the bush and busting up fences. But a guy in a four wheel drive ute, tanked up on beer, with a row of spotlights on his roof and travelling at crazy speeds through the forest at night is not only bloody scary, it destroys the bushland and frequently breaks down the riverbanks as well.

There, I got that off my chest!

That's why on the coming Thursday, the former school student sometimes known as TA was taking his swag and heading off to the bends for a spot of "me" time, and maybe also to think about what I'd do when the exam results came out.

"You got your meds, son?" It was Mum's daily mantra, which still managed to irritate me.

"Yes, Mum. But you do know that I haven't had a turn for ages and really..."

"I think you should listen to your mum, Tel." Dad's voice floated in from the shop, and with that the conversation ended – well, almost. "Kev's here to see you son."

For some reason my heart skipped a beat. Mums can pick this sort of stuff up easily in their kids.

"You OK, son? You sure you've been taking those tablets?" Genuine concern imbued her voice.

"Yeah. I'm fine, Mum. Maybe just a little bit excited," and I gave her a smile, a hug and a tickle which she hated! She made to flick me with her ever present tea towel but I'd left the house and was already in the shop.

"G'day, Kev."

"G'day, Tel. You going up to Gordon's Bends? Nice day for it. Tom asked me to give you this." He sniffed loudly as his eyebrows arched over his eyes like two bushy, black half-moons. He handed me a letter and without any more ado gave a parting, "See ya," and left.

Dad glanced across at me before continuing with packing fresh carrots into a neat stack for display in the shop. Nothing was said, not that I could have said anything even if he'd asked me. So I tucked the letter into my swag, shouted, "Bye, Mum," into the house and gave Dad a big, long hug before adding, "See you tomorrow, Dad." I felt his firm grip on my arm long after I'd turned off Lisle Street and was heading off towards the river.

That letter turned my mind into a whirlpool of thoughts and anxieties, so I had no recollection of anything that I saw along the track until I was well and truly close to my campsite.

It was the screech of some galahs that brought me back into the present. One of them was hanging upside down from a branch while another was sidling to and fro next to him, screeching at his antics. Mad as a galah – the accuracy of the description made me smile. For a fleeting moment I wondered why I assumed that it was the male who was upside down and the female bird screeching. You would never think of an owl doing anything like that. Now where did THAT thought come from?

I soon found my favourite spot and made camp. It was a bit late to fish, but I had nothing else planned, so I got my rod and some bait and sat on a fallen tree that lay half in and half out of the river. The trunk was polished by many a local backside, it being the perfect position for a good fish, and I spent a delightful hour or two flicking the float out into the river and watching it come back to me happily hopping in the eddies, and then dipping with the occasional nibble from an unseen mouth. But the fish weren't hungry, not that it really mattered. Come evening, they'd be dying to taste my juicy bait and all I needed was just one fish for a good feed.

Having exhausted myself from the exertions of float watching, I stretched out on my swag and took out Homer.

> *Now that royal Odysseus has taken his revenge,*
> *Let both sides seal their pacts that he shall reign for life,*
> *And let us purge their memories of the bloody slaughter*
> *Of their brothers and their sons. Let them be friends,*
> *Devoted as in the old days. Let peace and wealth*
> *Come cresting through the land.*

"Tel." I sat up and rubbed my eyes. At first I thought it was Kev, but then I realised it was Mentor. I looked around me to see where I was and yes, I was still on my swag and the dead tree was still lying in the river.

"What are you doing here?" I asked in genuine amazement.

"He's gone." The voice was instantly recognisable to me. Scrambling to my feet, there behind Mentor I saw the tearful face of Telemachus, son of Odysseus. My mind searched for some peg on which to hang a thought but found none.

"The gods said we should find you. They said you'd know why." Mentor, who was so like Kev it still made me wonder, put his hand on my shoulder, "but first Telemachus must tell his tale."

My namesake looked wrecked. He had dark circles around his eyes and he repeatedly pushed his black hair back from his face as if he were trying to push away some dense cloud from his mind.

"What do you mean, 'he's gone'?" I stupidly said. I glanced at my copy of Homer's *Oddysey* and tried to recall the exact ending. "But didn't your mum test your dad with the trick question about the bed when it was all over? And didn't they all live happily ever after when the suitors finally gave up after Laertes killed Antinous' old man with a spear?" By the look in Telemachus' face, it appeared that there was a gaping gap in my knowledge.

"I thought that was going to happen too, my friend," he said, gradually regathering the strands of his thinking. "Perhaps it was always what the gods had in mind. Perhaps it had never been intended the way I'd imagined it would be. Penelope herself seems not to miss his presence even though she loves him so dearly. Like my father, she is a great schemer and is endlessly patient. May I?" he asked, pointing to the ground next to me. Seeing my nod, he sat down and we both looked at the river as it flowed past.

"Everything was peaceful at first. The gods banished the memory of the slaughter from the minds of the suitors and their families, so peace returned to Ithaca. Our household was restored and replenished and my father travelled throughout his lands giving out orders and rewarding all those who had remained loyal through all the years of his absence." Telemachus brushed a bull ant from his leg, surprised by the size of the insect.

"Their bite is pretty vicious, too," I informed him.

"The gods find their emissaries in the most unlikely of places." He checked the ground around him before continuing his story. "Yet a cloud hung over my father. There had been a prophecy…" His voice trailed off and tears appeared in his eyes. "The prophecy said that my father should take an oar and travel throughout the land until he found people who did not know what it was."

A duck landed noisily on the river before gliding in silence near to the bank where we were. We watched the wake it created form rills on the water, which glinted with a silvered light.

"And now he's gone."

"I'm so sorry, Telemachus," I mumbled. "I know you miss him, especially after all the years you've waited for him to come home. But you know what? The world isn't what we think or imagine it to be, sometimes it's even better than we'd imagined. My parents adopted me when I was little, and in this letter," I rummaged in my swag to produce Tom's missive from Hazel, "are the names of my real parents." I looked at my friend with a sudden clarity of mind. "And I've been so stupid! I failed to appreciate what was right in front of my eyes."

I put my arms around his shoulders and said, "Go home. Be patient and your prayers will be answered. Odysseus will return. Go home to your mum, to your grandad, to your people and then one day, when you have a family of your own, you'll understand how difficult and lonely it can be to be a father sometimes."

He looked at me sideways as if a lock had been turned on a thought, which had suddenly released a decision.

Suddenly, a branch fell from one of the river red gums – it happened sometimes out there in the forest. River red gums are enormous trees and their branches are bloody huge, and when they drop off like that they make one heck of a noise. And if that wasn't enough to frighten the living daylights out of me, the noise from the cockatoos screaming in fright was! I even thought that I heard the hoot of an owl.

I turned my attention back to Telemachus, but he'd gone. Mentor was standing there with the setting sun shining brightly behind him.

"That was a big bastard. If it had happened a couple of minutes earlier it would have landed on mi' noggin."

"Kev?"

"Who'd you think it was, the Queen of Sheba?"

"What…?" words tumbled around in my mind like a bar room fight with no obvious winner.

"Just thought that you might like some company seeing as you've just got Tom's note."

The letter was still in my hand.

"Mind if I…?" Kev said as he sat down on the swag next to me.

At the start of the year I thought I was just like any other normal teenager, but since then all the anchors which had secured my life seemed to have been tossed overboard. But I felt a strange serenity amongst all the turmoil.

I stared at the envelope and smiled.

"Can I ask you a question, Kev?"

"Go ahead."

"Well, you remember that girl in Essendon, Mary, she was really cute. But then Julie's growing into a real good sort too. What do you reckon I should do?"

Kev seemed unperturbed by my question but his arched eyebrows suggested that he was considering my inquiry seriously. "Well, an old sheila I met once reckoned that young blokes need to fall in love at least nine times before they're likely to meet the right one."

"What about you, Kev?"

"I'm well into double figures, but that's none of your business, young fella." I joined him in his laughter as I dropped the letter into the embers of my campfire.

We both sat and watched as a black patch seeped into the white surface and a thin thread of white smoke drifted up out of it into the still air. Slowly the envelope flap peeled back and in the instant before it was engulfed in hungry flames, I saw the name of my parents.

I find my parents

THE JOURNEY DOWN to Melbourne was not for commercial reasons, it was to take me to Melbourne University to enrol as a law student. The day had started brightly with Mum fussing over me like the gorgeous Greek mum that she is.

"You be sure to eat good, Tel," she said, "None of that fried rubbish, plenty of good Greek places to eat in the city. Greek food is why we Greeks have best brains in the world." Her attempt at humour was to hide the genuine distress that she felt at her only child leaving home, probably for good.

Dad had lumped my hold-all and swag into the back of the truck as I hugged Kath and Mum goodbye. Those two ladies have degrees in crying, so it was good that they were together to comfort each other after I left.

"I'll ring as soon as I get settled. Love you Mum, Kath," and with a wave of my arm we set off up Lisle Street and out of Yarramah for only the gods knows how long.

We'd just left Benalla, where I'd told Dad about Kev's friend Phil and what a great guy he was, and how the Abs had been treated so badly, when a hiatus appeared in the conversation.

"What was it like back on the island you came from, Dad? From the stories you've told me it must have been hard to leave, eh?"

I thought that he gripped the steering wheel a little harder and shifted uncomfortably in his seat.

"It was a small island, much smaller than Ithaca." He smiled. "Life was pretty simple, I suppose. The family had lived on the same bit of land for generations. We boys helped Dad with the sheep, the olive grove and in the vineyard while the girls helped Mum and Granny out in the house and garden. We all went to the same village school, which was the only one on the island. There was only one teacher. Your mum went to it as well. She was in the year below, not that it made much difference as we were all in the same room anyway. She lived with her family on the other side of the village.

"Once we'd finished school though, there were no jobs for us, only work on the land. I don't think it's changed much, either. When you work for your family you don't get paid wages, you just get board and lodge, so if you weren't cut out for farming, there was no future in staying there. In the end, the only option for young people was emigration to America or Australia. I had uncles in Sydney, so I chose to go there. They were good to me and sent me the fare, so I was pretty happy to come. Australia's been really good for us."

"And what about Mum? Why did she leave?" This time his seat shifting was decidedly animated and I could see how hard this was for him.

I carefully put my hand on his on the steering wheel. "I know who my real parents are, Dad. It's OK."

Without taking his eyes off the road, he asked, "How?"

"Kev has a mate in Melbourne who found out for me." Dad said nothing. There was just the sound of the truck engine and the wind coming in the windows for a moment or two. "Remember that note he gave to me that time I went camping down at the bends?"

"Right." Another pause before he took a deep breath and briefly looked out the side window at the passing countryside. "Your mum and I had always been friends, still are." He smiled softly at himself. "As kids, there wasn't a time when we didn't see each other. We were together at school, at church, at weddings, birthdays, even funerals. She was my best mate, really.

"When it came time for me to leave, we went on a picnic down at one of the small beaches not far from the village. If there's one thing I miss about home, it's those beaches;

the white sand, the sound of the surf on the reef, the stars at night. So beautiful." His words were so evocative, if I'd closed my eyes I honestly believe I would have been there.

"It's a different beauty here. It's harsher, a bit more un-forgiving, but this is a land of opportunity for anyone with an ounce of energy in them.

"That evening we sat on the beach and talked and talked about the past and what the future might hold. I asked what she was thinking of doing when she finished school. She had aunts in Melbourne and was hoping to go there so we imagined that we'd be neighbours. Little did we realise how big this country is!" A Holden ute shot past us with a Bachelors and Spinsters sticker on the tailgate, the happy passenger shouting something incomprehensible at us. Dad smiled.

"It was such a beautiful evening and we were very, very happy. We held each as tightly as we could, just hoping that we might hold on to that moment forever. We really didn't know what we were doing." Dad paused, glanced out of his side window before almost whispering, "And the next day, I left."

He sucked in a deep lungful of country air. "There was no such thing as phoning home in those days. Everything was done by letter and that could take weeks or sometimes months to get a reply. After I got to Sydney, the first time I heard from Nana she'd already arrived in Melbourne. I was amazed and excited that she'd arrived here so soon after

I left. Then I read her letter and discovered why she'd followed after me so quickly. She'd written to tell me that she was pregnant – with you.

"One of the reason's she'd come was to avoid disgracing her family and bringing shame on them; the most important one, she wrote, was that she loved me, which immediately soothed my mind. Apparently she had no idea at first that she was pregnant, but her mum picked it up when she started being sick. Her mum is a good woman and in her heart would have loved for Nana to stay home. But the old rules and traditions still had an iron grip in our village and there was no choice other than she should leave the island immediately. At first I was really confused, then I felt a deep concern for her and deep in my heart, I knew I loved her."

Dad drove on in silence, remembering stuff that was in a different planetary system to my teenage mind. A couple of cars passed us by before he took up his story again.

"Your mum's got aunts in Melbourne. Good people who'd agreed to take her in and look after her until you were born, but then the family had decided to adopt you out."

My beautiful father turned to me and smiled, "There was no way I was going to let that happen to a child of mine."

"So what was with the whole charade about me being adopted?" I wasn't angry with him, but I just couldn't comprehend why anyone would take a baby away from its mother. "There was no need to do that. Why not just get married and make everything legit?"

"Shame," he said grimly.

Shame is such an ugly word and nothing good ever seems to come out of it.

"Family shame," he continued. "Even ten thousand miles away from home, shame has infected the suburbs of sunny Melbourne where so many Greeks now live. But it's not just us Greeks, it's the same with most other religions. They even teach it in schools by standing kids in the corner if they get a spelling wrong or can't do their times tables. And even footy supporters mock and shame their team if they lose or make a mistake.

"So we had no choice, really, we were just kids who knew nothing about the world and how could we make decent parents? That's the argument they used against us. In the end, we were forced to make a solemn pact with my uncles and Nana's aunts that we wouldn't do anything to bring shame on the family name. They even made us swear on the Bible. That's a terrible oath to take, but we did it because we held our family in such high respect.

"They told us that when Nana got close to the end of her pregnancy, she'd have to go and live with her Aunt Periboea in the country, and have the baby there. Secretly, they also made plans to have the baby adopted. These are good people who were trying to do the best by the family."

Dad looked at me and smiled.

"What they didn't know was that plans can be changed. Auntie Peri turned out to be one of the kindest people God ever placed on this planet.

"When it came close to the time for you to be born, I left Sydney without telling anyone and headed to Berowa, where Nana was. Aunt Peri took me in like I was her own son and fussed over the two us like we were newlyweds, which she also just happened to arrange shortly before you were born. She arranged a civil ceremony for us in Shepparton so that when you were born, you'd be legally ours."

"But why the charade about me being adopted, then? I don't get it Dad. Why didn't you tell me?" I pleaded.

"We'd sworn an oath on the Holy Bible to respect the wishes of our families. For all of us, that was, is, such a sacred thing." For a teenage kid with polished, passionate ideals, it was hard for me to comprehend what Dad was saying.

"It nearly broke your mother's heart. We were in such a terrible position, but what choice did we have? We both knew that we owed them so much and for our generation, it would be impossible break such an oath. As long as we had you, though, in the end we realised it wouldn't make much difference. We were going to be your parents. Would it really make much difference? No other people on this planet would ever be able to love you as much as we did, and still do."

The word 'but' was forming in my mouth, and then it seemed to dissolve and dissipate. A lightness of mood dawned in my mind. They loved me, they chose me twice and they never broke their oath. We drove on in silence towards our destinations.

"By the way," Dad said, rummaging around in the inside pocket of his jacket, "Kev asked me to give you this." He handed me a slip of paper from one of those small note pads with coiled wire along the top.

> *G'day Tel. I'm not much cop at writing so I'll keep it short. Tom knows a bloke who's in the medical line. Hopeless punter and owes Tom big time. He's a neuro-wotsit. Tom'll explain. Anyway, he should be able to check out your noggin' and see if it's in good working order. From where I'm standing, I reckon it should be OK. Kev.*

"The man's a genius," I muttered under my breath.
"Amen to that," said Dad.

Prophecy

*O*DYSSEUS MUST FULFIL *the prophecy of Tiresias, spoken at the Land of the Dead: The king must walk inland, from a foreign shore, carrying a well-planed oar until he finds people who know nothing of the sea. When someone mistakes the oar for a fan that winnows grain, Odysseus is to plant the oar and sacrifice a ram, a bull, and a wild boar to Poseidon. He can then return home, make offerings to the gods, and live out a peaceful life.*

Glossary,

and useful information for non-Australians

Chook Harris — *Bad man who came from out near Deniliquin. Pathological liar. Father a shearer and Mum a good person. May be a Catholic*

Yarramah Disctrict hospital — *where Tel was taken on each occasion he lost consciousness*

Julie — *Young girl in same class at school with Tel.*

Peter — *owns the fruit and veggie shop in the Lisle street, the main street in Byford dark brown eyes and black drooping 'mustache*

Kevin O'Ryan — *Owns the cement works in Byford. Single man and Tel's Mentor*

Dr Buckley — *local GP*

Jim Watt	*ambulance driver in Byford*
Furphy	*an erroneous or improbable story that is claimed to be factual*
Karrangatta	*Local big town where the Base Hospital is*
Sonny Liston	*Former world heavyweight boxing champion*
Carry on like a pork chop	*Behave like an idiot*
Dag	*Autralianism: an entertainingly eccentric person; a character*
sheila	*Colloquial word for a girl*
Lippy	*Short for lipstick*
Duffer	*Colloquial expression for acting like an idiot. Originally meant a sheep stealer*
Kath Connell	*Friend of the family - large lady who loved her smokes and her 'happy happies"*
VB	*Victoria Bitter - Australian beer*
Rigi dig	*Absolute truth*

Snagger	*Slang for a sausage*
Take no prisoners	*A term meaning she was a passionate supporter*
One eyed	*Biased*
Cockies	*Slang term farmers in Australia*
Paddock	*Term used for a footy oval or playing field*
Roos	*Slang for Kangaroos*
A hip and shoulder	*A form of tackle in Australian rules footy*
Roughie	*Raw talent*
The rough end of the pineapple	*Suffered some bad luck,*
Took a mark	*Caught the ball from a kick*
Arvo	*Slang for afternoon*
Awen	*A real presence, almost like an aura*
Boof head	*An idiot*
Mick	*Slang term for a Roman Catholic*

Yabbie	*A fresh water Crustacea found in Australia*
Barbie	*Short for barBque*
Snags	*Slang for sausages*
Rellies	*Slang for relatives*
Soak up the rays	*Sun bake/sunbath*
Off spider	*Helper or assistant*
a few tiles short of a roof."*	*Simple minded*
sussed	*Suspected*
toe-ey	*Unstable, upset*
Dill	*A fool, not quite all there*
Fr Brian	*The new local curate - 6' 4" and overweight*
Leggies	*A slang term for a "leg break" which is a form of bowling in cricket*
Blow-in	*A stranger in town*
Mozzies	*Mosquitoes*

Bulldust   *Fanciful, a lie, a deception*

Porky pies   *Lies*

Vinnies   *Members of the St Vincent de Paul's Society*

Mick   *Slang for a Roman Catholic*

Bums rush   *Told him to clear off*

Up to snuff *Good enough to perform a task*

Dag   *Clown, fool*

Peri   *Short for Periboea*

Noggin   *Head*

Furphy   *a rumour or story, especially one that is untrue or absurd.*

About the Author

"I spent all my life learning the rules. Now that I know which ones are irrelevant, life is simpler!"

AFTER MORE THAN thirty years as a busy family practice physician in Perth, Duncan Jefferson retired from his practice and started traveling. He still practices medicine part time, as a relief doctor traveling to the most remote corners of Australia, and in between assignments he and his wife travel the world.

Duncan has walked the famous Camino de Santiago, and now volunteers his time as the chairman of The Pilgrim Trail Foundation, which is organizing a similar, contemplative-style walk in Australia called the Camino Salvado.

VISIT HIM ONLINE AT

WWW.DUNCANJEFFERSON.COM